A SLASH OF COLOR

An Ami Dautry Mystery

Carol Rifon

CR Press   Cottonwood, Arizona

A SLASH OF COLOR
Copyright © 2022 by Carol Rifon

All rights reserved. No part of this book may be reproduced
or transmitted in any form or by any means without written
permission from the author.

ISBN-13 978-0-9841719-3-4
ISBN-10 0-9841719-3-2

**All characters in this book are fictional and are not
representative of any real persons living or dead.**

Dedication

To my husband, Charles Riggio

Special Thanks

To Karen Hatler for her exceptional proofing abilities

Table of Contents

CHAPTER ONE

The Departure

"Looks like you sold almost everything," said Marianne. She assessed the few garage sale items left on the table and added, "We'll have just one small box for Goodwill."

"Glad to see it all found a home. I feel lighter already," said Ami, flopping into a lawn chair and flinging her arms in the air.

"I wish you weren't moving so far away. I'll miss you."

"I'll miss you, too, Dear," returned Ami. She held great affection for her niece. Despite the almost thirty year age difference, they had become good friends. "But it's time, and it makes sense." Her husband, George, had died two years ago and six month ago her daughter, Shirley, and family had moved to Oregon. "I'll be closer to Shirley and Granny." Her mother, who was in her seventies, lived in Monterey.

Marianne walked across the yard and sat next to her aunt. "I promised I'd do this, so here goes. Shirley called me last night and asked me to try one more time to convince you to move in with them."

Ami turned with a stern expression. "I have already made it clear to her I do not want to do that. I will not discuss this again."

"Okay. No discussion on your part. I'll talk and you listen."

Ami smiled despite herself. It was so like Marianne not to be deterred from her mission.

"Shirley said since you refuse to live with them permanently, would you consider staying with them for several months while you search for a house in California?"

"No!" answered Ami with defiance.

"I don't blame you for refusing," sympathized Marianne. "I wouldn't want to stay with her either. She's so much like my mother, it's scary! They're both narcissists, probably mixed with OCD. And that's just the start of the diagnosis."

Ami laughed. "I thought you hung up your shingle a couple years ago. Aren't you into feng shui now?" Ami's reference was to Marianne's recent switch to yet another topic of study. Ami had experienced, over many years, Marianne's habit of submerging herself in a passion of study, inflicting that information on everyone around her and then capriciously dropping it for a new interest. Mike was the constant in Marianne's life. They had been married for six years. Ami was pleased and impressed by his tenacity.

"There is an underlying psychology to feng shui, too," continued Marianne, "but that's another story. When I tell her you won't stay, her next request will be for you to visit before flying to California. We both know that's so she can try to guilt you into staying."

Ami sighed. "I love my daughter, and would give my life for her."

"But?" interjected Marianne.

"But since George died, she's become more controlling than ever. I hate to say this, but I don't enjoy being around her. Even staying with her on that short visit over Christmas was barely manageable."

"With Uncle George gone, she thinks she has to take charge of your life now. You do realize your refusal is driving her crazy?"

"I know. I have to confess that I'm enjoying my rebelliousness," admitted Ami.

"I'm loving it! And I'm really proud of you for not buckling under," praised Marianne.

"Thanks, Dear. My decision to move closer to them makes sense, but my life must remain my own."

Ami had made the decision to revitalize her life with a new environment and new people and new experiences. She felt if she remained in Seashell Beach or moved in with her daughter, she'd feel trapped in the past. She had allowed herself to grieve fully for George. Her daily sadness now was replaced with thoughts of happy memories. She felt a connection with George's spirit and knew he'd be angry if she stopped living just because he was dead.

"What do you want me to tell her?"

"That I have made other plans."

"What plans?"

"I'll tell you if you promise not to give Shirley the details."

"Promise with pleasure!" agreed Marianne.

"I've confirmed my reservations at a bed and breakfast in Cypress Nest."

"Where's that?"

"It's a pretty little coastal town about 60 miles from Granny. George and I drove through it about six years ago on one of our visits. We stopped there for lunch and really loved the feel of it."

"What's it like?" asked Marianne with interest.

"Well, I expect it's changed since we were there, but it seemed quiet and artistic, mostly theater I think from all of the postings around town. Yesterday, out of the blue, the memory of Cypress Nest suddenly popped in my mind." Ami pulled out her cell phone. "I went online and there was this guest house for sale!" She handed the phone to Marianne.

Marianne moved through the link and studied the floor plan. "It's lovely. It's small, but the light wooden floors and large windows give it an open feel. Nicely designed deck. Great ocean view."

"I called the listing broker and arranged to see it next week. I hope it's as nice as the photos and is still available."

"I'm sure it will be. It's your new home. It's perfect for you!"

"Your optimism is daunting," said Ami.

"I know. It's my superpower!" claimed Marianne, flexing her biceps. "Okay, I'll call Shirley and tell her staying with them is out. They have your dog and that's all they're getting."

"Oh, I do so miss Luke," uttered Ami.

"That was really unselfish of you to let him go."

"It was the right thing to do for both of them. Luke was pining miserably for George. When Teddy came to visit, Luke came alive again. Teddy was miserable about moving away from all of his friends. When I asked him if he wanted to take Luke to Oregon, his face lit up. Luke made moving bearable. It all worked out for the best."

"You know, Shirley is going to call my mom and list a dozen ways I should have approached you better. Did you know they video chat once a week complaining about us? It used to be mainly about me, but since your refusal to move in with Shirley, you're the hot topic."

"No, I didn't know that, but they're two peas in a pod, so it makes sense. Would you rather I talk to her?" offered Ami.

"No. What they think doesn't affect my life, but your moving does. I'm really happy for you, but I'm really sad you'll be so far away. I'd move to California in an instant. I can work anywhere I can charge my laptop, but Mike's tied to the office. Ooh, maybe Mike can get a transfer and we can move to Monterey near Granny. I love it there and it would only be about an hour or so from you," said Marianne, excitedly.

"Please, promise me you won't pressure Mike about moving. The poor man has enough stress trying to deal with you."

"Very funny. By the way, I want you to know that when you come back for visits, our beach house is your home for however long you want it. With us here only on weekends, you'd have lots of privacy."

"Thank you, Dear. That's very generous of you. But I doubt I'd visit very often. Hopefully, I'll have my California house soon and you can visit me."

Marianne scrolled through the photos again. "This really is a lovely home. Let me know the minute you have a move in date so I can arrange a flight out to feng shui it."

"You're getting way ahead of yourself. I haven't stepped foot in it yet. And even if it does work out, that's too long of a trip just to decorate a house."

"No, it's not. I'd love to come!" said Marianne enthusiastically. "I can spend a week doing your house and then a few days with Granny before flying home. Did you know Granny smokes pot now?"

"Granny has always smoked pot," informed Ami.

"You're kidding!"

"Almost every Saturday night, a distinct aroma would emanate from our parents' bedroom. Even as kids, we knew what it was. Your mother hated it. She said it smelled like skunk."

"What do you know? Granny really was a hippie. Well, she's legal now," dismissed Marianne. She scanned through the photos one more time before handing Ami back her phone. "I really love your new house."

"I may not end up buying this particular house."

"Oh, you will!" said Marianne wide eyed. "Uncle George instigated it. That's why Cypress Nest popped in your mind like that. He wants you to have it."

"Are you clairvoyant now?"

"I'm telling you, this is definitely your house!" insisted Marianne. "I think you should buy all the main pieces of furniture before I come out. That way, we'll only need to shop for accessories. I'll arrange them according to a feng shui bagua that creates peaceful energy. It's important that you start off your new life by creating the best possible atmosphere."

"I haven't even seen this house yet. So, don't get too excited," cautioned Ami.

"Come on, you can't tell me you aren't even a little excited about it."

Ami reached over and squeezed Marianne's hand. "I have to admit I'm feeling optimistic." She let go of Marianne's hand, sat upright and straightened her shoulders. "But we need to be realistic and not set our hearts on it, just in case it doesn't work out."

CHAPTER TWO

The Arrival

"Hi. I'm Ami Dautry."

"Oh, it's Amy, not Ami."

"My mother was studying French when I was born and thought it clever to spell my name with an "i" instead of a "y." It's been a bane my entire life."

"Well, I'm Meg Morgan. My mother was not clever. Welcome to Ocean View Real Estate." She reached out and shook Ami's hand.

Upon touch, Ami felt an instant connection with this tall, attractive and well-dressed woman. "Thank you," replied Ami with a warm smile. Ami's eyes were drawn to Meg's earrings. They were huge. She'd never seen any quite that large. Somehow, they seemed a natural fit for this woman who, Ami guessed, was in her late fifties.

"Can I get you a bottle of water before we head out?" offered Meg.

"No, thanks."

"Then, let's do it! I know you're anxious to see the house."

"Well, I'm certainly curious about it," replied Ami.

"How was your trip?" asked Meg, as they walked toward the parking lot.

"Best part was flying into Monterey. It's such an easy airport to navigate. And the drive to Cypress Nest was just beautiful."

"We're so spoiled. I just hate whenever I'm forced to go to LAX." Meg unlocked her BMW and Ami slid into the passenger's seat.

"When did you arrive?" asked Meg as she pulled out of the parking lot.

"Three days ago. I'm staying at a lovely bed and breakfast up the road."

"Oh, Cypress Cottage. I agree, it is lovely. And aren't the gardens wonderful?"

"Yes!" answered Ami with exuberance. "Such a diversity of plants and flowers. Somehow they've created what appears a garden growing naturally, yet perfectly manicured."

"Oh, that Bill Arnold is amazing. He designed the gardens himself. Meticulous about detail. Has an excellent full time gardener, but, often, you'll catch Bill out there up to his elbows in mulch. He was a well-known LA interior designer, retired now.   Did you notice his exquisite antiques?"

"I noticed the beautiful furniture and accessories, but I'm not knowledgeable about antiques."

"Well, I am and I can assure you he has no reproductions. Very impressive collection."

"I'm impressed by his staff. They have the perfect balance of being professional, helpful, and friendly. I'm thoroughly enjoying the accommodations."

"Enjoy now because I doubt you'll be staying there long.   This house is ready for immediate occupancy. You're going to love it!"

"We'll see," replied Ami. Despite the fact she was trying to act nonchalant, Ami's stomach was filled with butterflies of excitement.   From the moment she had checked into Cypress Cottage, she had felt comfortable with the area. It felt like home here.

"Did you have an opportunity to hear Josh play?" asked Meg. "He's a famous musician, you know?"

"Josh played for us one night and it was obvious he was talented. I didn't know he was famous."

"Oh, we have a number of celebrities living in Cypress Nest. Elise Foster from the soap *The Proud and the Powerful* is retired here. As a matter of fact, not only is she your neighbor, but she's the seller of your house. It used to be her guest house.   Last year, she totally remodeled it as a surprise for her twenty year old daughter. Only her daughter had other plans. Eloped last month with an Australian soccer player and moved to Australia. Surprisingly, Elise took it rather well. She tends to be a diva. Not in a bad way, just theatrical. Anyway, that's why the house is available for you."

Ami smiled at Meg's preemptive completion of the sale. Oddly enough, Ami was feeling a sense of ownership herself, and she hadn't stepped foot in the door.

"I think you'll find Elise a good neighbor and a lot of fun. She's in Australia at present. She stars in many of our local plays. She also produces, along with Sharon Hart Randall."

"I'm afraid I don't watch daytime television, so I'm not familiar with either of them."

"Sharon's not a celebrity. Not nationally, anyway. She has some fame around here as the local wealthy widow. Married four times. Each husband wealthier than the next. Lovely lady. Tragic story though. All her husbands died shortly after she married them. She's vowed never to remarry."

"Famous musicians, soap stars, wealthy widows? I'm afraid I won't fit in." Ami was beginning to feel intimidated and wondered if she'd make any friends. She didn't seem to have anything in common with any of the people Meg had mentioned so far.

"Nonsense! You're a well-known portrait artist!"

"How do you know I'm an artist?"

"Easy, Honey, I checked your on-line profile. You'll fit right in. Of course, fitting in means getting involved with the Cypress Nest Theater. It is the center of all activity here. Almost everyone either performs or supports the theater in some way. I'm sure they'll be clamoring at your door for your artistic talent. Unless you're interested in performing?"

"No performing for me. But I enjoy the theater and would be willing to participate as an audience member."

"I'm with you. I figure someone has to be in the audience, so I'm in the front row of every performance cheering them on. Here we are." Meg pulled the car to a smooth stop.

Ami stepped from the car and stood in the driveway assessing the small house. It was just as welcoming as the computer photos hinted. Nicely pruned shrubs were tucked snuggly under the front windows. A gnarled Cypress tree graced the front yard. It was so beautifully formed it seemed unreal. The white trim of the front porch shone crisp and refreshing. Ami sighed with relief. It was lovely.

Meg unlocked the door. She had a big grin. "If you like the outside, you're going to love what's in here!"

Ami hurried up the drive and followed Meg inside. It was an open room with light colored wood flooring. She was awed by the vastness of the ocean visible through three panels of glass facing her. The center panel was a French door that led to the outside deck. The windows and door were framed in light wood like the floor. The wood was attractive, but more importantly, grounded the room and helped contain the expansive view. The peach undertone of the off white walls brought warmth and safety to the room. Ami hadn't realized from the online posting that the kitchen and dining room were part of this space. Somehow, she had the impression they were separate rooms.

"Great view, isn't it?" asked Meg with a grin.

"Yes. Somewhat overwhelming, actually," admitted Ami.

"Oh, you'll learn to appreciate that!"

"The room is lovely and bright with the windows and vaulted ceiling. It has a stone fireplace," said Ami walking to the wall opposite the windows.

"It's gas and easy to maintain," informed Meg.

Ami strolled around the room. "The floor space itself is rather limited though."

"I grant you it isn't large enough for a grand piano, but it's plenty generous for entertaining. And you can easily extend the floor space by opening the doors to the deck." Meg walked over and opened the French doors. "See?" She stepped onto the deck and raised her arms in the air. "Roomy, isn't' it?"

Ami followed Meg out to the deck.

"It runs the whole width of the house and can be accessed by French doors here, and doors from the master bedroom and one of the guest rooms," informed Meg.

The deck was much larger than Ami had initially realized. It certainly would expand the entertaining area. Of course, having no friends here, whom would she entertain? She was sure she would make friends eventually. Meg seemed friendly. Certainly, her goal was to sell Ami a house, but Ami felt comfortable with Meg. Ami had painted portraits long enough to know that the eyes reflected a person's inner qualities. Meg had honest eyes. Ami felt sure Meg was trustworthy. Walking around the deck, Ami found herself satisfied with the floor space.

"Your property is an eighth of an acre. Think of yourself as a little diamond in the center of all these large homes. Your neighbors are 200 yards away on either side." Meg pointed to homes right and left. "There are no empty lots. Their property adjoins yours, which means you'll continue to have plenty of privacy. Your property extends twenty-five feet from the end of your deck, basically to the end of those rocks. The rest is public beach. Although, you'll rarely see anyone but locals at Cypress Nest. Too many rocks and too short of a beach for tourist traffic."

"The view is wonderful! I'm surprised at the noise though. I lived at the beach back East, but had to walk to the ocean. The ocean is much louder than I expected when it's at the door."

“Oh, you’ll get used to that!

Ami followed Meg back into the living room.

“And the house is so well insulated you can turn down the volume by closing up the windows.” Meg flipped a switch on the wall and outside white metal blinds automatically rolled down and enclosed the house in darkness. The house was silent.

“That’s convenient!” stated Ami, impressed.

“It’s a privacy feature Elise had installed on all the windows and French doors. She didn’t want her daughter to be bothered by the press.” Meg flicked the switch and raised the blinds.

Ami looked across at the kitchen. “I didn’t realize from the photos that the dining room and kitchen were part of the same room. I don’t know that I like seeing into the kitchen from the living room.”

“I hear you,” assured Meg. “The open kitchen causes you hesitation. I take it you haven’t had an open floor plan before.”

“No, I haven’t,” said Ami.

“The open kitchen concept is so convenient and social, perfect for welcoming your guests to participate in preparations or to sit at the counter, sip a drink and visit while you cook. The counter is granite. Isn’t the waterfall island beautiful?”

“It certainly is, but I’m still not sure.”

“Well, you can think about it. Let’s go check out your master suite. Come see how plush it is!” said Meg brightly, leading Ami to a recessed archway to the right of the living room.

“That door on the left goes to the garage,” advised Meg. “And this one leads to serenity and comfort.” Meg swept the door open with panache.

The master suite was filled with light. It was on the small side, but could handle a king bed, and the French doors opening onto the ocean deck made it appear larger than it measured. Meg opened the French doors and they walked out to the deck. "Can't you picture yourself lounging out here in the ocean breeze before bed?"

Ami pictured that easily.

Returning to the bedroom, Ami opened the closet. It was a small walk in with built in shelves and drawers. The efficient design used up all the space and provided a good deal of storage.

"The jewel of this house is the remodeled master bath," said Meg. She opened the door and stood aside to give Ami full access.

"Oh, my!" said Ami walking into the room. Serious thought had been put into this room. It was luxuriously designed. A sunken spa tub sat next to a large window overlooking an ocean view. Over the tub was a skylight. Beautiful tile work adorned the shower and toilet enclosures. And the exquisite crystal wash basin was a work of art. Ami had seen more modest versions of baths like this in design magazines. Although she had secretly dreamed of luxuriating in a spa tub, she was far too practical to have made it a priority in house hunting.

"Can't you just visualize yourself soaking in that tub, enjoying the view?"

"Oh, yes," agreed Ami rapturously. She quickly tried to cover her awed response by changing the subject. "What about the guest rooms?"

She noticed that Meg smiled knowingly.

They walked out of the master suite, across the living room to a small alcove on the left side of the house. There were three doors; guest rooms on each end and the center led to the guest bath.

The guest bath was nicely appointed with both a shower and a tub. Both guestrooms were sunny with views; one of the ocean with a door leading to the deck, the other of the cypress tree in the front yard. Ami considered them small but suitable for guests.

As they returned to the living room, Meg led Ami to two doors near the garage alcove. Ami expected they were closets.

Meg opened one of the doors. "This powder room was remodeled along with the master suite bath. Isn't that washbowl elegant?" asked Meg.

"Indeed, it is," agreed Ami. As with the master bath, the powder room had a carved glass washbowl. This one was a dolphin design in sea blues and greens. The inset lighting accentuated its beauty. It was a tiny, but functional, room.

"This is laundry center!" Meg said, opening the second door. "You have space saving stackables. Notice the built in hamper, convenient shelving and handy drying rack. And look at this," Meg opened a wall cabinet and flipped down an ironing board, "Ta da! If you do that sort of thing," she added.

Ami laughed. "I try to avoid it."

"Me, too! If it's not wrinkle free or dry cleanable, I don't buy it!" Meg flipped the ironing board back up and closed the door. Let's check out the garage."

Ami followed Meg into the garage. The garage was a medium-sized, one-car with finished walls, nice shelving, pegboards and narrow workbench. It would do nicely.

"And last but, by far, what I'm guessing will be most important to you," teased Meg, "follow me."

Ami followed Meg to the right side of the back deck and down a few stairs. Beside the deck was a ten by ten foot windowed and enclosed gazebo. Meg opened the door and they went inside the light-filled room. "Elise had it built as a yoga space for her daughter. What do you think of it as an art studio for you? It has north and west light."

"Perfect," sighed Ami. She felt overwhelmed. This house was amazing. Ami decided she needed to regroup. "I'd like more time to study both the inside and outside of the house. What's your time schedule, Meg?"

"Don't worry about me, Honey. I give my clients lots of time. My car is like a mini office. I'll just go out and make some calls. You take all the time you need."

"Thank you, Meg," replied Ami gratefully, relieved to have some time alone.

Ami walked around the gazebo. It was perfect for her studio. Having a studio outside her door with an ocean view was beyond her dreams. Leaving her studio at the art mall in Seashell Beach had been the hardest part of moving.

She ambled around the deck checking the wood for deterioration. She walked throughout the house several times, checking the faucets in the bathrooms and searching for leaks under the sinks. Everything in the house looked new and freshly installed. Settling on one of the stools by the waterfall island, Ami reassessed the kitchen more closely. The cabinets were roomy and solid wood, stained to match the woodwork around the French door and windows. The appliances were attractive and efficiently designed. She realized that her initial concern about the open floor plan was her unfamiliarity with it, always having had individual living, dining and kitchen areas in her other homes. She found her resistance fall away. The ability to enjoy a magnificent ocean view from anywhere in the room was amazing. She smiled thinking of how much Marianne would love it. She decided she liked the house very much, especially the master bath with that luxurious spa tub. The house was perfect. More importantly, it felt comfortable. It felt like home.

She opened her purse, took out her cell phone and pulled up a photo of George. "What do you think, George? Oh, I know it may seem foolish to buy the first house I've seen, but it's the smallest house in the neighborhood and that's the only reason buying here is a possibility. There aren't many affordable beach homes here. Not that this one is affordable! But I have your life insurance and the sale from our house and the inheritance from Uncle Joe. Point is, I like this house, George. It feels like home. And I like this community. I'm aware I don't know anyone yet. But it feels right to me. Now, you know I'm no fool. I'll pay an inspection company to come in and check everything with a magnifying glass before I finalize the sale. But it's obvious to see it's just been remodeled. What do you think, George?"

She put her hand over the photo and closed her eyes. After a few moments, she opened them. "Thanks, George," she said and put the phone back in her purse.

She walked out the front door, down the sidewalk and turned to gaze at the house. Initially, she had felt it welcome her. Now, with the sunlight shining brightly around it, it seemed a happy home. She walked to the car and got inside. "Meg, let's go back to your office and put in an offer."

"Honey, I knew this one was yours the minute I met you!"

Ami offered her a crooked smile, and they both began to laugh.

CHAPTER THREE
The Visit

Marianne had announced upon her arrival the night before that she planned to spend two weeks rather than one. Her project was to feng shui Ami's home. She had briefly toured the house before falling into bed, exhausted from travel. Upon awakening, she had spent most of the morning and afternoon traversing through Ami's home making lists of accessories to buy.

"I can't believe you bought white leather loveseats!" said Marianne settling herself into one of them.

"You don't like them?" asked Ami.

"I love them! And I love that your dining table matches the color of the flooring and the white dining chairs are just the right size. All the pieces are perfect for this space. I just didn't think you'd buy anything this contemporary."

"Thanks for the backhanded compliment," replied Ami, flopping into the other loveseat.

Marianne laughed. "It's just totally different from your other house, yet it suits you. You were right to sell all of your old stuff. None of it would have fit in here. I love the neutral palette. It makes the space appear larger. And it allows us to use color as accent, and for you to change it when you want a new look."

"That's exactly what Bill said. The neutral white and matching wood tones were his idea. He also suggested the loveseats in lieu of a sofa."

"Who's Bill? He has good ideas."

"Bill and Josh own Cypress Cottage. That's the bed and breakfast where I stayed for a month while buying the house. They were very kind to me. Bill has created a beautiful garden there. You can see it tomorrow when we stop by. I think you'll enjoy discussing your plans with him. He was an interior designer in LA."

"No wonder he gave you such great advice."

"I'm pleased you like everything," said Ami.

"Well, there is one problem piece of furniture we need to discuss. That single bed of yours is bad feng shui," said Marianne.

"That bed is the most expensive piece of furniture in this house. It's completely adjustable and has three massage settings. It's the most comfortable bed I've ever owned. I've been sleeping like a baby. I'm not giving it up," insisted Ami.

"You don't need to give it up. You need to get another one to put beside it."

"I only need one bed to sleep in," said Ami.

"But what if you had a guest spend the night? Where would he sleep?" posed Marianne.

"I have a two guest rooms."

"I'm talking about a guest you'd like to sleep beside," emphasized Marianne.

"I don't plan on a guest of that nature," informed Ami.

"Love is one of the keys of feng shui. By maintaining a single bed, you are blocking love from your life. It's necessary that we get a second bed in there."

"I don't agree, and even if I did, it would throw us way over budget."

Ami had given Marianne a budget to help curtail her exuberance. Their agreement was Marianne had creative freedom until it was time to actually purchase something; then Ami would make the final decision.

"It will be my house warming gift to you."

"No. It's far too expensive. Most importantly, I have no use for it," insisted Ami.

"Not yet, but you will. It's important that you create energy for opportunities."

"I don't want to talk about this anymore. Come on, let's go sit outside!" said Ami.

Marianne opened the French doors and walked out onto the deck. "Just look at your view! Aunt Ami, this house is much more beautiful than the website photos. Ahh, this is wonderful," said Marianne kicking off her sandals. "I bet you're just loving it!"

Ami settled into the chair next to Marianne's. "I've only been here a month, so I'm still settling in. But I am happy."

"I'm happy for you." She smiled at her aunt. "Now, back to business, tell me about the shops around here? Where did you get those loveseats and that dining suite?"

"Little shop downtown. Meg Morgan, my real estate agent, told me about it. Her friend, Julie Crestly, owns it. Julie carries mostly accessories, but she had lots of catalogs of good quality furniture and ordered it all for me. She saved me a lot of time. Oh, I'm painting her portrait. She came over a couple days ago for her initial sitting."

"Your first commission since you've been here! How exciting!" announced Marianne appreciatively. "Your studio is perfect, by the way."

"It is, isn't it?" beamed Ami. Her easels and art supplies were the only things Ami had shipped to her new home.

"Well, it sounds like you're meeting people and making friends."

"I've met a few people, but I can hardly call them friends yet. I take that back. I would consider Bill and Josh new friends. I like them and enjoy their company."

"Tomorrow, let's tap Bill for suggestions about accessories," said Marianne.

"No!" objected Ami. "He's retired."

"You didn't mind him giving you all that other styling advice."

"He volunteered that information when he and Josh toured the house after I bought it. Asking him would be taking advantage of a new friendship."

"You said I could get his opinion on my ideas. That's where I'll start. During our conversation, I'll prod him for suggestions and advice. You won't be taking advantage. You'll be an innocent bystander with a pushy niece. Was Josh a designer as well?"

"Josh is a talented musician. Major player in the local theater guild. Wrote two original musical scores for them. Also, the headliner at local charity concerts."

"And Meg and Julie have become your friends."

"Meg, yes. We spent a good bit of time together while I was moving in. Now, we meet about once a week for lunch. She's quite a character. Wears enormous earrings. Somehow, they look perfectly appropriate with her big personality. You'll love her. As for Julie, I'm not sure. I like her and she's friendly. But her naturally bossy nature is a little much for me. She's also a big wig in the local theater guild. Meg said Julie is a take charge kind of person who has no patience with the members who don't pull their weight. Apparently, some of the members are involved just for the status. Meg called them leeches."

"Can't wait to meet Meg. I like her already! What about your neighbors?" Marianne gestured to the houses on either side of Ami's.

"To our right," Ami pointed to a large two story home with blue trim, is my famous neighbor, the TV star."

"Ooh, What star?" cooed Marianne.

"A retired soap star named Elise Foster. Actually, this used to be her guest house. She renovated it for a daughter who eloped with an Australian soccer player. Hence, it went on the market and I got to buy it. I haven't met Elise yet. She's been in Australia visiting her daughter. Supposedly, she's returning today in time for Sharon's party tonight. Sharon owns that enormous house next to Elise. Meg said Sharon Hart Randall is famous for her over the top parties.”

“I know who Elise is. She played Theadona Tilton on *The Proud and The Powerful* about five years ago. One of my college roommates was hooked on that show. I couldn’t get into it myself. Elise is a leggy blonde with big boobs. Well, she was on the show anyway. So who lives in the big tan house to the left?”

“That’s Lou’s house. Retired engineer. Made his fortune through inventing some kind of manufacturing gizmo. Widow. Nice man. Had me over for brunch last week. Lovely home.”

“Had you to brunch? Just the two of you? Reee…ally? You may need that second bed sooner than I thought,” teased Marianne.

“Believe me, neither of us is interested. He spent half the time reminiscing about his dead wife and the other half prattling about Elise. He said Elise is interested in my painting her portrait, so they’ve obviously kept in touch while she’s been away. We’ll see if she approaches me once she’s back home. Meg said Elise and Lou have a hot thing going. I think he really cares for her. I hope she cares back. I’d hate to see him get hurt.”

“You sound very protective of someone you just met. Sure there isn’t some interest there?” probed Marianne.

“Very sure. I was touched by the loving way he talked about his wife, Lucy. They were married for thirty years. She died five years ago. He said before he asked Elise on their first date, he went to Lucy’s grave and asked her permission. I totally got that. I talk to your Uncle George every day, and I asked his opinion before I bought this house. I know it sounds crazy.”

“I don’t think it sounds crazy at all,” said Marianne. “I think it’s sweet.”

Ami smiled at her. "We better start getting ready for the party." Amy's invitation had included a guest, making her comfortable bringing Marianne along.

"Can't believe I'm going to a fancy party my first day here. I'm excited to meet all of these people!" bubbled Marianne.

"I'll be meeting many of them for the first time as well. I consulted Meg about dress. Seems everyone dons their best silks and gems for Sharon's parties. Did you bring anything fancy to wear?"

"Sorry. My mink cape is in the wash and my diamond tiara is out on loan."

"I'm being serious. These people will be dressed to the nines."

"Aunt Ami, I promise to fit in. I always travel with a pair of black dress slacks and a silk tunic. I'll cinch a silver belt over the tunic, pull my hair up in a puffy knot and fancy it all off with a pair of dangling earrings. I'll be simply breathtaking!"

"I bought what I think is an appropriate dress," announced Ami nervously. "It's an ankle length, blue chiffon with a V neckline that's modest, but it does show a hint of cleavage."

"Does the V reach your belly button? Do your boobs spill out into view?" asked Marianne.

"Of course not!"

"Then, you'll go unnoticed. If the soap diva dresses anything like her character, she'll be wearing something sexy and dripping in diamonds. She'll draw all the attention. You can relax."

"I suppose they'll all be wearing those lavish gems Meg mentioned," said Ami. "Well, my diamond earrings and single diamond pendant will have to do."

"Why are you letting these people intimidate you? I've never seen you worry about stuff like this before. If clothes and diamonds are all that matter to them, they aren't worth your friendship."

Ami took a deep breath. "Thanks, Dear. I needed to hear that."

Marianne put her hand on Ami's arm. "What is going on with you?"

"I admit I've been feeling insecure all day," confessed Ami. She looked into Marianne's eyes. "When you arrived last night, I was so happy to see you. It made me miss my old life. It was comfortable and safe with lots of friends and lots of work. Seeing you reminded me that I'm alone here. I've moved across country, to a place where I know no one, and bought a guest house in rich people's land. Suddenly, I feel scared and lonely."

"Anyone would be if you look at it that way," sympathized Marianne. "But I'm impressed by what you've done! You bravely moved forward into a new phase in your life. You found and bought this amazing house with a studio right outside your door. You already have a commission for a portrait. And you've made three fast and great friends. I can't wait to meet them!"

"You're right. It's all a matter of perspective. It's what I wanted and it's going to work out," stated Ami.

"Of course, it will," agreed Marianne.

CHAPTER FOUR

The Party

"Ami, you look beautiful," said Bill smiling. "And this must be your lovely niece."

"Yes. Marianne, this is Bill Arnold."

"I've heard so much about your magnificent garden. Can't wait to see it," said Marianne. "By the way, the furniture pieces you suggested for Aunt Ami are perfect!"

"I'm so pleased you like them. Ami mentioned you're studying feng shui and are here to help her with energy flow through the house. Why don't you stop by tomorrow for brunch and we'll exchange ideas?"

"I'd love to!" gushed Marianne.

"And I love that you're a fellow long legs," he whispered to Marianne. He turned his attention to Ami. "Being the petite belle that you are, Ami, you have no idea how tall people suffer. The back of my neck and shoulders ache after the constant pressure of looking down all evening."

"I'll second that!" agreed Marianne. "At least we'll get to look each other in the eyes."

"We pair nicely," suggested Bill.

"Okay, now that we're friends, I'd like some insight on these people judging my aunt. Who can she trust and who should she avoid?"

"Marianne!" chided Ami.

"Let her alone," said Bill. "Her youthful honesty and enthusiasm is refreshing. And I love to gossip, so what do you want to know, mon très cher?"

"I want to know if Ami will dance with me," said Josh, joining them with a smile. "You must be Marianne."

"Yes. And you must be Josh Boston, the famous musician. Nice to meet you."

"I noticed you and our lovely hostess were gone awhile. She guilted you, didn't she?" asked Bill.

"Yes. It's only one song at the upcoming hospital charity event," informed Josh.

"Which she knows will turn into encores and that's why she baited you with one," stated Bill.

"Naturally," said Josh.

Bill turned to Ami and Marianne. "Let me explain what we're talking about. Sharon Hart Randall, our beautiful hostess, uses her parties for one-on-one meetings to ask for favors. Not for herself, mind you, but for her charities."

"She's on every board in town and contributes generously to all of them," added Josh, "but she often requests what her money can't buy."

"And she just asked you to donate your time and talent," said Marianne.

"Yes," he answered. "I don't mind. It's for a good cause."

"The sticky wicket," said Bill, "is that the good causes seem endless."

"Enough petty complaining." Josh reached for Ami's arm. "Ami, I insist you come along with me. We'll enjoy our dance while they enjoy their gossip." Josh twirled Ami's arm over her head and spun her away. He glanced back and winked at Bill.

"How did he know we wanted to gossip?" asked Marianne.

"Elementary, my dear. I'm the biggest gossip in town and you're fresh meat."

"Okay, then." Marianne leaned into him and whispered, "Our rich widow hostess is dancing around the room with enough rubies to cause an insurance adjuster a heart attack. I assume they're real; is she?"

"Yes. As we mentioned, Sharon is a generous contributor to many charities. Her personality tends to be upper crust, but, aside from that, she's a genuinely nice person. Her parties and dinners are over the top, but she has so much money and expensive jewelry, she has to create excuses to use them. Tonight, you'll notice a change of dresses and gems several times throughout the evening. She's currently wearing her second fashion statement."

"You're kidding!"

"Not at all. She lives in a bubble of excess. Extravagance is her norm. But she has a sense of humor about it. Hence, the sign up sheets in the foyer."

"Yes, what about that? When we arrived, her secretary instructed us that the sheets numbering one through five were for the dress changes Sharon would make this evening. To play along, I signed up for three and Aunt Ami for four. So, what's the joke?"

"No joke. Each person on the winning list will receive $10,000 toward the charity of their choice."

"I've never heard of anything so strange. Is she mentally sound? Meg told Aunt Ami all her rich husbands died shortly after she married them. Did she knock them off?"

"You're shocking! And such fun," appraised Bill. "Sharon is astute and money savvy, but a romantic. I believe she loved them all, making her saga rather sad. Her first marriage was to a wealthy Brit in line for some minor title. They were married a little over a year when he was smacked in the head with a mallet during a polo game. Died of a brain hemorrhage, so, no, she didn't kill him. Husband number two lasted three years. He dropped dead from a congenital heart condition at mama's house, so no, she didn't kill him either. The third was a troubled two-year marriage to an east coast tycoon. Got drunk, fell off his yacht and drowned. Sharon was not aboard, but a curvaceous blonde was, so no. The fourth, and richest of the bunch, was a French investment banker. She was married to him the longest, a little over five years. Died of lung cancer, so no."

"What about the tuxedo adhering to her? That woman in the green dress keeps eying them with envy. Which one is she interested in?"

Bill laughed loudly causing a few partygoer glances. "That's a complicated story," he whispered.

"I'm listening."

The waiter arrived just then with a fresh tray of champagne and they each took a glass. A second waiter arrived with a tray of canapés. Even though the waiters circled continuously, Marianne stuffed one in her mouth and stacked two more in a napkin in her hand.

"The tux is Arthur Tusko, old money, super rich, and Sharon's current partner." Bill took a sip of champagne before continuing. "Previously, he belonged to the green dress. That's Julie Crestly, local business owner, theater board member, all around bossy lady."

"Aunt Ami is painting her portrait," said Marianne, biting into another canapé.

"Really?" questioned Bill.

"Yes," said Marianne swallowing. "She had her first sitting a couple of days ago."

"Interesting," softly hummed Bill.

"You think she's having it painted for self enjoyment, the tux or that blonde cutie staring at her from across the room?"

Bill cocked his head, "You're a quick one."

"Thanks!" she said, smiling. "Aunt Ami's portraits aren't cheap. My bet is on self enjoyment. Can't imagine her spending that much on an ex or the cutie since he's across the room and not with her. Who is he?"

"Jerry Robson, professional tennis, ATP top one hundred, recently stopped touring, bad shoulder and he turned thirty-six. Arthur's step-son from a previous marriage. Jerry and Julie have a troubled relationship. His obvious absence at Julie's side tonight is telling."

"Wait! Julie was an item with the step-father and now with his step-son?"

"Yes. We're a regular *Peyton Place.*"

"A what?"

"Ahh youth! *Peyton Place* was a book, movie and TV show about a scandalous community," explained Bill. "I thoroughly enjoyed them all."

Marianne laughed, "Not surprising. So tell me more about this love triangle. Is Julie trying to rekindle with Arthur now that Jerry is no longer pulling in big tennis bucks?"

"No, my delightful one. Even without his tennis income, Jerry has enough money from his grandfather's trust to last several lifetimes. I assure you, there's no triangle there. Neither Julie nor Arthur want to rekindle that relationship."

"Bad breakup?"

"Not at all. Very amicable. Their parting was simply a matter of different interests. Julie's interests overwhelmed Arthur's inclinations. He is a much better fit for Sharon."

"Then, why the envious stares?" Marianne popped the last canapé into her mouth.

"I think Julie envies their relationship. Arthur and Sharon are content. Julie and Jerry struggle to find harmony. The evil sour note is her daughter, Crystal. That's Crystal over there, covered in sequins."

"She's pretty if she'd stop scowling. Who is she angry with?" asked Marianne.

"Most likely her mother, or Jerry, or both."

"Crystal doesn't like Jerry."

"Au contraire, mon tendre. Elle l'aime trop. She wants him for herself. Hence, the love triangle for which you asked."

"Talk about a daddy complex. He's twice her age. She's just a teen. Doesn't her father object?"

"Crystal's parents divorced when she was a child. She's twenty-four. Gets botox."

"Really? Already?"

"Not unusual for this group."

"Still, you have to agree he's a better fit for the mother," asserted Marianne.

"I do agree. And to Jerry's credit, he's openly and clearly stated his love for Julie, but Crystal refuses to accept it."

"So why don't Jerry and Julie just tell Crystal to butt out? Aunt Ami said Julie is a bossy lady."

"Julie is bossy with everyone *except* Crystal. Indulges her. Appeases her. Acts like her lapdog."

"Why?"

"Because Crystal throws tantrums if she doesn't get what she wants."

"What a little witch!" asserted Marianne.

"Don't you think the 'b' word is more accurate?"

Marianne laughed. "I love you."

"Feeling is mutual."

"Hey, take a look at Aunt Ami and the hunk she's dancing with."

"Hunk?"

"Well, you know, an age-appropriate hunk. I'd like to see her in a relationship," confided Marianne.

"Animated conversation. Both smiling. Looks like mutual attraction. It's possible," assessed Bill.

"Who is he and is he single?"

"Lucas Dawson. Local police chief. Yes, he's single. As a matter of fact, he's one of our closest friends. I have no hesitation recommending him."

"I'm guessing he's divorced," said Marianne.

"Five years ago."

"How come?" asked Marianne.

"Lucas and his wife moved here from LA where all of her friends and family lived."

"I get it. She missed them and wanted to go back," said Marianne.

"Yes. And she missed the activity of big city night life. Lucas was happy to be away from all that. She wanted out. He let her go. Clean break."

"How long had they been married and did they have any kids?"

"Seven years and no."

"That's only twelve years and he looks about fifty. Was he married previously?"

"You're quiet an interrogator. I admire that. I find you thoroughly enjoyable, mon très cher."

"Thanks!"

"Lucas is fifty-six. No previous marriages. He was too busy focusing on his career to marry young."

"What's his dating history since?" asked Marianne.

"Mostly casual. He hasn't clicked with anyone. His focus is always on work. But he certainly seems interested in Ami. I'm so pleased."

"Ooh, this sounds promising," cooed Marianne. "I was hoping she'd meet someone tonight. Hey, the players in our love triangle have disappeared!"

"You're right. Jerry and Julie probably tried to slip out. My guess is Crystal followed them."

"I think Crystal suffers from daddy abandonment issues and blames Julie. Her attempt to take Jerry away from her mother is her way of hurting mama back. Julie's catering to Crystal is Julie's attempt at making up for divorcing the father. Basic psychology," said Marianne.

"Oh, what insight have we here?"

"Before feng shui, I studied psychology. Before that, herbology. Before that, martial arts. Before that, massage therapy. I can go on and on. I enjoy learning new things."

"So you're a Renaissance woman."

Marianne's face went blank.

"That's a compliment," said Ami, walking up behind her. "It means you're interested in many fields of study."

"I certainly prefer that term to my family calling me scatterbrained."

Bill stared at Ami with reproach.

"Not Aunt Ami," interjected Marianne quickly. "I was referring to my parents. Well, just my mother."

Bill bowed his head. "Forgive me, Ami, for prejudging you."

Josh arrived with a glass of champagne for Ami. "Ami, you must be parched after all the dancing. I hope you're enjoying yourself."

Before she could answer, Meg joined them shouting, "Ami! Happy to see you! You look beautiful!"

"Thanks, Meg," replied Ami, taking a sip of champagne.

"Hi, Meg!" greeted Bill and Josh. "You're a late arrival," continued Bill.

"Oh, we got held up with the architects over the new resort addition. Then the minute we drove up, Julie approached. She's been upset all day. When Jerry joined us, Carl and I happily made our escape," sighed Meg. "You must be Marianne."

"I'm so happy to meet you, Meg. What bodacious earrings! I love them!" complimented Marianne.

"Bodacious describes me perfectly, Honey." She winked at Marianne. "Oh, where are my manners? Marianne, this is my friend, Carl Williams. He's a real estate developer here in Cypress Nest."

"Nice to meet you," said Carl, nodding to her.

"And you," said Marianne, nodding back.

"Anyone notice the outfit number? I signed up for four," said Meg, smiling.

"This is number three," informed Bill. "It was emeralds with black organza, rubies with white silk, now sapphires with navy crepe. My guess is she'll conclude the evening with diamonds. Looks like you and Ami will win."

"OMG, those sapphires are huge!" noted Marianne.

"They were a recent gift from Arthur," informed Meg. "And that's nothing compared to her diamonds. She's got some so big I don't know how she stands upright."

"Okay, Meg, what's going on with Julie and Jerry?" asked Bill. "They stayed apart all evening, looking heartbroken."

"Wretched situation," said Meg, shaking her head sadly. "Crystal went into a rage this afternoon over Julie and Jerry coming to the party together. Threatened to kill herself if Julie didn't give her Jerry."

"I doubt Jerry would be flattered to know he's being viewed as a commodity," noted Josh.

"Julie called Jerry and told him, for Crystal's sake, she was coming to the party alone. Jerry told her he's fed up with the drama and called it quits. Julie was crushed. She loves Jerry, but Crystal comes first."

"I don't see how anyone can blame Jerry," said Bill. "He's been more than patient with them. You dodged a bullet, Carl."

"I know," he responded.

Meg moved closer to Marianne. "Initially, I set Carl up with Julie. He's a nice guy and she's my friend. Well, they didn't click. And during the few dates they had, Crystal was extremely rude to him."

"Why didn't she like Carl?"

"Carl, tell Marianne why Crystal didn't like you."

"I wasn't old money like Arthur and Jerry. But it turned out for the best because now I'm with the woman of my dreams."

"How can I help but love him?" asked Meg, touching his arm tenderly. "So tell us about your work, Marianne. Ami said you're a graphic arts designer for video games. That sounds really interesting."

"Excuse me for interrupting, but did you say you're a gaming artist? That's my field! Well, my field of interest."

"Marianne, this brash young man is Matty Westford," introduced Meg.

"I'm sorry for interrupting," apologized Matty. "I heard video games and couldn't help myself. It's my dream job. I'm currently studying computer programming and graphics. Everyone says it's a hard field to break into. Do you have any connections?"

"Really, Matty!" chastised Meg.

"It's okay," said Marianne. "I can see you have a passion for it. Have you built your portfolio?"

"Yes. I've redesigned two of my favorite games and I've written and storyboarded two of my own."

Marianne reached into the pocket of her slacks, pulled out a business card and handed it to Matty. "I'll be here for two weeks. Give me a call and I'll look at your portfolio. If you're exceptionally talented, I may be able to get you an interview for an internship."

"Thanks! That sounds great!" Matty looked down at the card and then back at Marianne. "You're Marianne Eckhart? You designed TriangleTarget! Wow! It's like meeting gaming royalty! This is so great!" He grabbed her hand and shook it energetically.

Marianne laughed.

"Matty, what are you fussing about?" said Crystal, joining them.

"Crystal, this is Marianne Eckhart! She created TriangleTarget! And she's willing to look at my portfolio!"

"So, she's a computer nerd. Come on. I want to leave. Now, Matty!" called Crystal, walking away.

"I've got to go, but I'll call you. Thanks again."
Marianne nodded.

"Ami, I had no idea your niece was royalty," stated Meg.

"Guess I should have worn my tiara," said Marianne, laughing.

The rest of the group joined in.

>=<

"That party was a lot of fun," said Marianne as they walked out onto Ami's deck. "I liked your new friends a lot, especially Bill," said Marianne plopping down into a lounge chair, kicking off her shoes and wiggling her toes. "My feet hurt from standing in heels all night, but I'm not tired at all."

"I'm glad you enjoyed the party, Dear," said Ami, sitting down beside her.

"Didn't you?"

"Sure."

"Doesn't sound like a sure. You weren't still worried about your dress and jewelry were you? You looked beautiful. And your dress was modest."

"No. I had let all that go before we got there."

"So, what didn't you like?" asked Marianne.

"I didn't dislike anything in particular. It just isn't my kind of party. I prefer an intimate group of friends to big parties with idle chatter," said Ami.

"That's what I liked about it. I had a great time listening to all the gossip and studying people without being noticed. Too bad you didn't enjoy it more."

"There were parts I enjoyed. Specifically, Josh introducing me to everyone. Those one-on-ones were valuable. Now that I've been introduced, I'll feel comfortable waving or approaching someone when I'm out and about."

"You seemed to enjoy dancing."

"Yes, I did enjoy that. I've always loved to dance."

"I noticed you dancing with that handsome police chief. You seemed to be enjoying one another's company. Maybe he could become the love of your life?"

"I was married to the love of my life."

"I know, but he could be a new love."

"I'm not interested."

"Too bad. I'd like to see you get back in the game. Anyway, I thoroughly enjoyed myself. I loved talking with Bill! He was a wealth of juicy gossip. That love triangle with Julie and Crystal is soap opera worthy. By the way, our wealthy hostess did not kill any of her husbands. Can you believe she changed dresses and jewelry four times? That diamond necklace at the end was unbelievable! Do you think she had body guards mingling around the room protecting her?"

"We can discuss all of this tomorrow. Right now, I need to relax. I'm going to make myself a cup of herb tea and sit out here for awhile enjoying the quiet. Want tea?"

"No thanks. I'm feeling antsy. The moon is full and the ocean is calling. I'm going to walk along the beach."

"Do you want a flashlight to see down the stairs?"

"Don't need one. Moon is plenty bright enough. I'm just going to change."

While Ami made her tea, Marianne went to the guest room and changed into a sweatshirt and leggings. She slipped on her running shoes to be sure footed on the rocks at night.

"I'm leaving now," said Marianne from the deck by the guest room.

Ami was sitting on the deck by the living room. "I'll keep an eye on you while you walk and wait here until you get back."

"Okay, mother hen," Marianne shot back as she descended the stairs to the beach. As she reached the bottom step, she noticed something on the rocks. She walked over to get a better look. She leaned down, then backed away and ran up the stairs toward her aunt. "Aunt Ami!" Marianne shouted. "Call the police!"

Ami met her at the top of the stairs. "What's happened?"

Marianne took a moment to catch her breath, more from shock than exercise. "It's Julie Crestly. On the rocks. Dead."

CHAPTER FIVE

The Police

"Thank you, Mrs. Eckhart," said Chief Dawson. He looked out the door at Ami sitting on the deck. "I'll take a statement from your aunt now and then we won't need anything more from you this evening."

"Mrs. Dautry, may I join you?" asked Chief Dawson, opening the French doors to the deck.

"Of course," answered Ami.

"Would you care for some coffee or tea, Chief Dawson?"

"No, thanks."

"Tell me about tonight," he instructed.

"I have little to tell since it was my niece who found Julie."

"Can you detail your interactions with Mrs. Crestly at Mrs. Randall's party tonight?"

"I spoke with her early in the evening, but our time together was brief. Most of my evening was spent with Josh. He was introducing me around. After which, I spent some time dancing. I ended the evening talking with Marianne, Josh, Bill, Meg and Carl."

"Did you notice what time Mrs. Crestly left the party?"

"No. I noticed she had not been in the room for awhile, but didn't note the time she left."

"Was there a reason you noticed her absence?"

"As an artist, I notice colors and textures. Julie was wearing a beautiful green dress. It was distinctive in color and texture. I noticed the absence of the dress in the room."

Chief Dawson nodded. "How well were you acquainted with Mrs. Crestly?"

"I was just beginning to know her. Meg introduced us. After I purchased some furniture Julie ordered for me, she asked me to paint her portrait. She came to my studio this past Wednesday for her initial sitting. She was here approximately two hours," detailed Ami.

"Was anyone else present at the time?"

"No. Normally, the subject is alone, especially for the initial sitting."

"May I see the portrait?" he asked.

"Of course."

Ami led him to the studio.

"There's no lock on this door," noted Chief Dawson.

"No. It was designed as a yoga studio. I suppose I should have a lock installed now that I have art inside." Ami turned on the lights. The portrait sat on an easel in the center of the room. "Oh, no!" exclaimed Ami. She ran over to the painting and touched the canvas lightly with her fingers. There were deep, diagonal slashes across the portrait from right to left.

Chief Dawson moved forward and examined the slashes. "Is anything else in the room disturbed?"

Ami looked around the studio. She kept it neat and tidy. Everything appeared in place. "No. I don't think so."

"Excuse me a minute." Chief Dawson went outside and spoke to one of the other officers.

Ami stared at the painting. She felt broken hearted. She stamped her foot to keep from crying. Her eye caught something sparkly she must have kicked. She looked down at a couple of sequins.

Just then, Chief Dawson returned. "Let's go back up on the deck," he instructed.

He held Ami's arm, guiding her back to where they had been sitting.

"Mrs. Dautry, I can't help but notice that you're shaking. Are you concerned for your safety due to the slashed painting?"

"No. The fact that Julie's dead leads me to believe the slashing is expressing anger with her, not me."

"Astute observation. In that case, can I assume your distress is due to the destruction of the painting?"

"Yes. To an artist, a painting is a living thing. This portrait was just beginning its life. Like a baby beginning to babble. Now, it's dead. That's emotional," she explained.

"You mentioned earlier that you have a process when painting a portrait. I'd like to hear about it, especially now."

"My process begins before the subject has their first sitting. We meet to discuss their expectations and how they want to be portrayed. For example, their preference for formal or informal, focus on a hobby or talent, details as to the setting, their clothing, etc.? We also discuss the message they want to send. How do they want others to see them? How do they want to see themselves? What qualities do they want to shine through? Some people have very specific visions; others haven't even thought about it. I listen and note what they say. I study them as they talk. Then, I honestly respond as to how I can or cannot include what they want into the portrait. That takes about an hour or two."

"Is that the meeting you had with Mrs. Crestly when she was at your studio on Wednesday?"

"No. We had that meeting several days prior to her first sitting. Julie chose to come to my studio for her sitting. Most subjects prefer their own location, usually a specific room in their home and a personal prop."

"A prop?"

"Yes. Like sitting by their fireplace, or among flowers in their garden, or holding a racket by their tennis court. They prepare themselves with the clothes, jewelry, makeup, etc. that they want portrayed in the painting."

"Mrs. Crestly didn't do that?"

"No. She preferred to wear a business suit and sit here at my studio."

"During our dance at the party, you mentioned how subjects don't sit for hours anymore. You said you take photographs."

"Correct. The subject positions himself how he wants to be portrayed and I take about two dozen photographs from various angles."

"Had you taken photographs of Mrs. Crestly?"

"Yes."

"I'd like to see those photographs," he directed.

"They're on my computer. I can download them to a flashdrive for you. Do you want it now?"

"No, tomorrow is fine. Thank you. What was the next stage of your process after you had taken the photos of Mrs. Crestly?"

"She sat for a short sketching session. I began with a brush and thinned paint, focusing strictly on placement, not detail. I washed in some values, but at this early stage, the white of my canvas served as the light so it went quickly. In less than an hour, she had left."

"What was the process after she left?"

"After that first sitting, I worked on my own in my studio, adding more detail and a little more color. That's as far as I got with Julie's portrait."

"Had the process proceeded, what would have been the next step?"

"I would have blocked in the color with thicker paints. That's when it actually begins to look like a portrait."

"When would Mrs. Crestly have come for another sitting?"

"She really wouldn't sit again. Location, dress and position are done and I have the photos. I would have met with her two more times. After the block in, I would have invited her to my studio to view her portrait and discuss if it was on track with her expectations. This can take ten minutes to an hour, depending on the discussion. Once we were in agreement, I would have worked on my own again, completing the portrait. The third and final meeting, usually in my studio, is to focus on facial nuances that might need adjusting. If needed, I make them at that time. Once the portrait is dried, I would have delivered it to her." Ami sat back and relaxed in her chair. She felt exhausted.

"That was helpful in allowing me to understand process and time frames. I appreciate your detailing it for me."

"I suspect a side motive was an effort to divert my attention and calm my emotions. Thank you."

"I see nothing gets past you. So, who do you think would want to deface your portrait of Mrs. Crestly?"

"I don't know any of these people well enough to form an opinion at the moment."

"Thank you. That's all for tonight. We'll be here awhile longer. The steps to the beach and your studio will be a cordoned off. You can move about the house and deck freely."

Ami got up from her chair and walked into the house.

Marianne was sitting by the fireplace. "Your neighbor, Lou, stopped by. He saw the police and wanted to make sure you were okay. I told him what happened. He said your soap star neighbor is still in Australia."

Ami walked across the room and sat on the opposite loveseat to Marianne.

"You look like you're in shock. Do you want a brandy or something?" asked Marianne.

"Surprisingly, I do," Ami answered.

Marianne got up and poured a little brandy into a snifter. She handed it to her aunt and sat back down across from her.

Ami took a sip of brandy before she spoke, "Someone slashed Julie's portrait."

"Aunt Ami, I'm so sorry. That must have hurt you deeply."

"Yes, it did." Ami set her glass on the coffee table. "I'm going to bed. I'll tell you more in the morning."

"Goodnight," said Marianne. She picked up her aunt's glass, took a sip of brandy, leaned into the loveseat and sighed.

CHAPTER SIX

The Brunch

"Hello," said Marianne answering her cell phone.

"Marianne, it's Bill Arnold. We heard what happened. Instead of your coming here as planned, Josh and I will be over at eleven with brunch. We want you and Ami to know we're here for you."

"Thanks, Bill. That's thoughtful of you. And, I suppose, you want to see the scene of the crime."

"It seems you know me too well, too soon. See you then, mon très cher."

"Who was that?" asked Ami coming out of her bedroom.

"Bill Arnold. He and Josh are bringing us brunch at eleven. I hope that's okay with you," asked Marianne.

"Sure. It's kind of them." Ami walked to the French doors and looked out onto the deck.

"The police are gone," informed Marianne. "I've been out there looking around. They've got tape on the steps and your studio door. I made coffee. Do you want some?"

"I'm going to jump in the shower and dress first. I'll be out shortly," said Ami, leaving the room.

>=<

Bill and Josh walked back into the living room from the deck.

"I didn't know I'd feel so sad seeing that," said Josh. "It's just tape, but the inference is so sinister."

"Isn't it though?" agreed Marianne.

"Ami, I'm curious as to why there is tape on your studio door?" asked Bill.

47

"The killer went into her studio and slashed Julie's portrait," answered Marianne. She placed some salmon on a bagel half and bit into it. "This is yummy. I'm starving."

"Eat up, mon très cher," urged Bill.

"Slashing the portrait seems like some sort of warning? Are you in danger?" asked Josh.

"I don't think so," dismissed Ami.

"You are both to come and stay at the B and B as our guests until the police make an arrest. We intend to protect you," said Josh.

"That is very thoughtful of you, but we're perfectly safe here," assured Ami. "Whoever slashed the portrait was angry with Julie, not me."

"Isn't slashing the portrait overkill? Pun not intended," said Bill.

"I think the portrait was slashed first. This was all about rage. It wasn't thought through," said Ami.

"So you think Julie's murder wasn't planned? It just happened?" asked Josh.

"Yes," answered Ami.

>=<

Marianne and Josh had just finished putting the last of the leftovers in the refrigerator when multiple rings of the doorbell startled them.

Josh ran to it and look through the peep hole. "It's Meg and Carl," he informed. He opened the door.

"I'm shocked. I can't believe it," Meg said entering the room.

Josh hugged her. "I'm so sorry, Meg. I know Julie was your dearest friend." He escorted her out to the deck where Ami and Bill were sitting.

"Sorry to barge in," said Carl, following them, "but Meg needed to see where it happened. She's been crying all morning."

"Come with me," said Bill taking her hand. "Don't go past the taped areas," he instructed. He guided Meg and Carl toward the stairs.

While they were gone, Josh quickly helped Marianne prepare a tray of cheeses, fruit and bagel cubes. They opened a bottle of wine and carried it out to the deck.

Meg returned to the table and collapsed into a chair next to Ami. "I can't believe she's dead." She took a tissue from her purse and sopped up the tears running down her face.

Josh handed her a glass of wine.

"Thanks. Keep it flowing. I just want to stay numb and pretend it's not real."

Carl sliced a small piece of cheese off the wedge on the table and popped it in his mouth. "How are you holding up, Ami? Lousy welcome to the neighborhood, isn't it? I'm sorry."

"I'm sorry for you and Meg. I know what it's like to lose someone you love," said Ami.

"Thanks, Honey. I appreciate that," said Meg. She pulled another tissue from her purse and blew her nose.

"I assume Lucas informed Crystal," said Josh. "Meg, have you been able to talk with her. This is devastating news. How is she handling it?"

"You tell them," urged Meg to Carl. "I'm too bitter."

Carl patted Meg's hand. "Meg called Crystal and expressed sympathy. Asked if she needed anything. Her response was rather nasty," explained Carl. "She informed Meg to leave her alone. Said she planned on selling the house and business, and use a realtor other than Meg. Made some statement about being free and independently wealthy now. Not a word of sadness over Julie."

"Maybe you should notify Lucas that his chief suspect plans to escape," said Bill.

"Suspect? You don't really think she'd kill her own mother to have Jerry do you?" asked Marianne.

"I do," admitted Carl. "Crystal was banging on Jerry's door first thing this morning."

"Are you serious?" asked Josh.

"Yes. I called Jerry to check on him," said Carl. "I knew he'd be broken over this. He loved Julie. He told me Crystal repeatedly called his cell all morning. He didn't answer so she left messages telling him she loved him and they could be together now. I guess she got tired of his not answering his phone, so she went to his house and banged on the door. He didn't respond or let her in."

"Good for him!" said Bill. "This is what happens when you indulge and spoil a child. They grow up to kill you."

"Crystal seems immature so maybe she's acting out to block the grief of losing her mother," suggested Marianne.

"It's kind of you to defend her, but you needn't bother," advised Meg. "Crystal is acting like the spoiled brat she's always been. Julie overindulged her. It encouraged Crystal to become more and more demanding."

"I suspect Crystal is serious about selling Julie's business. I doubt she's interested or capable of managing it. Is she, Meg?" asked Josh.

"Crystal has never taken an interest and hasn't a clue about Julie's business. Of course, a good realtor and accountant can help guide her through the sale."

"You don't honestly believe Crystal will listen to anyone?" asked Bill. "And her foolish statement about being independently wealthy is telling. It will be months before Julie's estate is settled. She has no access to her mother's money. Does she have money of her own?"

"I don't know. Matty says Crystal has a lot of money hidden in different banks, but I doubt that since Crystal constantly complained of being broke and needing money," said Meg. "In addition to the extra money Crystal asked her for, Julie made generous monthly deposits to the bank account she had set up for Crystal."

"Julie can't deposit additional funds now, so Crystal is on her own," noted Bill. "She may have to resort to actually finding some employment."

"Crystal has a credit card that Julie gave her," said Meg. "I guess she can use that for expenses. But if she's on drugs, like Julie has long suspected, she's probably maxed it out."

At the sound of the doorbell, they all turned.

Marianne went to answer it. She looked through the peep hole, then ran back to the deck. "Speak of the devil. It's Crystal!" she whispered.

"Well, answer the door, please," instructed Ami.

Marianne walked to the door and opened it. "May I help you?"

"I came to see your aunt."

"May I tell her what this is in reference to?"

"No. Just get her."

"I'll see if she's available. Please wait here."

"She's right there. I can see her." Crystal pushed Marianne aside and walked past her to the deck.

"Hey!" shouted Marianne, following her.

"I came to inform you," said Crystal, staring at Ami, "that I'm not paying for that portrait of my mother."

"I want nothing from you," answered Ami.

"She paid you already, didn't she? I thought so. Well, I want that money back. You give it to me right now!"

"There is nothing to give you and nothing I want from you. Please leave," calmly stated Ami.

Crystal grabbed the cheese knife from the table and pointed it toward Ami. "You give me that money. Now!"

Reactively, Marianne twirled, extended her leg upward and kicked the knife from Crystal's hand. Another twirl and kick met Crystal's head, knocking her to the floor. Crystal didn't move. She was out cold.

"I knew one day those martial arts classes would come in handy," said Marianne.

No one spoke.

>=<

After Crystal had been examined by the paramedics, booked and removed from Ami's house, and Chief Dawson had taken each of their statements independently, he sat down at the table with the group.

"Lucas, are you off duty now?" asked Josh.

"Hold on," said Bill. "You're not off duty yet. I have this for you." Bill handed Lucas a cell phone. "It's Crystal's. Her password is 42669," said Bill

"How do you know that?"

"I asked Marianne to figure it out for me. Took her less than a minute. She's a wiz."

Lucas looked across at Marianne.

"It was a no brainer," she said. "Lots of people substitute letters for numbers so all they have to remember is a word. Passwords reflecting a current passion are common. I just typed in JERRY and it opened. Most cell passwords are child's play."

"Where did you get this phone?" Lucas asked Bill.

"I found it under the table. My guess is it fell out of her pocket when Marianne kicked her and she hit the floor. I'm ashamed to admit it, but I froze when Crystal grabbed that knife and threatened Ami," said Bill.

"Don't be hard on yourself. We all froze, except for twirling legs here," said Meg. "Honey, when you started twirling and kicking, I thought I was watching something on TV. I'll never forget it. You were amazing!"

"You are the hero of the day, mon très cher!" said Bill.

52

"Thanks, but now that it's over, I'm worried," admitted Marianne. "I know the paramedics said she was okay, but Crystal threatened to sue me for knocking her out. Last night, Mike was upset when I told him I found Julie's body. Tonight's video chat will be another shocker for him. He's really going to be upset that we might get sued!"

"Don't worry, Honey," said Meg. "We've all given statements to what happened. We're reliable witnesses. It's clear you were defending Ami. We'll stand by you. You did good."

"Thanks. Gee, I'm feeling really shaky." Marianne sat down heavily.

"Would you like a Vicodin?" asked Meg, reaching in her purse.

"No, thanks. I don't want opioids," said Marianne.

"Oh, Honey, they're not dangerous. We all use them for pain. Most of us use Vicodin. Jerry opted for Percocet. He needed something a little stronger for that long standing shoulder injury," she explained.

"You'll be okay, Marianne," assured Lucas. "You're feeling the adrenaline crush. It's a post adrenaline rush blood sugar drop. It can take awhile to even out. The more you relax, the quicker that shaky feeling will subside and you'll return to normal." He picked up the bottle of wine from the table, poured a little in a glass and handed it to Marianne. "Take a small sip of wine and a couple of slow, deep breaths," he advised with a kind smile.

Marianne nodded and smiled back at him.

"By the way, Lucas, Crystal has some interesting texts on her phone," said Bill. "The one to Jerry this morning follows what Carl mentioned about the phone calls. It celebrates the fact that they are finally free to begin their new life together. Is that enough evidence to arrest her for suspicion in Julie's death?"

"Of course, that hateful brat did it," said Meg.

"I assume Jerry ignored the text, like he did with her phone calls this morning," said Carl.

"I didn't see a response from Jerry," said Bill.

"Bill, I am directing you to refrain from talking about anything you saw on this phone. Is that understood?"

"Oh, come on, Lucas."

"Bill?"

"Understood," agreed Bill.

"Thank you."

"Off duty, now?" asked Josh of Lucas, holding up a glass of wine.

"Yes. Thank you," said Lucas, reaching for the glass. He looked over at Marianne. "How are you feeling?"

"Better," she said. "Thanks."

He nodded to her.

Josh placed a tray of sandwiches on the table. "Here, self serve. We have roast beef on grilled baguette and salmon on brioche. Condiments on the side."

"When did you do all this?" asked Meg.

"I called earlier and asked Mary to prepare something for us. Nick just delivered it."

"I want to know how Mary gets these beef slices so thin," said Carl. "Delicious."

"She chills the roast and uses the deli slicer," enlightened Bill. "Makes the meat melt in your mouth."

Josh returned with a platter of brownies. "Mary sent these along as a special treat," he said, placing them on the table.

"Josh, your thoughtfulness is beyond measure. Thank you," said Ami.

Lucas leaned close to Ami. "I believe those are the first words you've spoken all afternoon. Are you okay?"

"Yes. I'm afraid I've been off in my own little world."

He studied her for a moment. "Your first month with us certainly has been an intrusive one, hasn't it, Ami? May I call you Ami now that I'm off duty?"

"Of course," she answered.

"Although it doesn't seem so, I assure you our community is a peaceful one."

"Could have fooled me," she said.

CHAPTER SEVEN

The Suspects

"Good morning, Aunt Ami. How are you feeling this morning?"

"More like myself."

"That's good to hear. Want some coffee?"

"Yes, please."

"Go out on the deck and I'll bring it to you."

Marianne carried two mugs and a plate with scrambled eggs, toast and fruit. She set the plate and one of the mugs in front of her aunt, and sat down beside her.

"You made me breakfast? That was kind of you." Ami dug her fork in hungrily.

"You were very subdued yesterday. Everyone was chattering away, and you hardly said a word. I've been worried about you."

"I'm sorry I worried you, Dear. I think I was stunned by the terrible things happening at my beautiful new house. My new life seemed tainted and sad. But I feel much better this morning," said Ami, continuing to eat her breakfast.

"That's a relief. What changed?"

Ami put down her fork and took a sip of coffee before she answered. "Last night, your Uncle George came to me in a dream. He was standing on the deck by my bedroom. He told me to follow him to my studio. I did; in my dream, not in reality. There was a gauntlet in front of the studio door. He told me to pick it up."

"You mean like that phrase 'take up the gauntlet'? What is a gauntlet anyway?"

"It's a glove."

"A glove? Really? I thought it was some kind of club."

56

"No. It's a protective glove. I picked it up and looked at him. He smiled at me and disappeared."

"That's such a powerful dream! Ooh, he's telling you to fight. To defend this house and your new life."

"I think so, too." said Ami. She picked up her fork and continued eating.

"So how do you do that?"

"I've decided to do whatever I can to help the police with Julie's murder. The sooner it's resolved, the sooner this tragedy is no longer on my door step."

"I'll help! Where do we start?"

"Obviously, with Crystal. I believe she slashed the portrait and killed her mother."

"She tried to kill you, too!"

"She tried to scare me into giving her money. If she really intended to kill me, she wouldn't have chosen a cheese knife in front of five witnesses."

"I don't know. Her behavior is erratic and she's desperate for money. And if she really is hyped up on drugs, who knows what she'd do?"

"At present, I can't prove she killed her mother, but I'm pretty sure I can prove she's the one who slashed the portrait."

"How?"

"When Chief Dawson and I were in the studio, I noticed a couple of sequins on the floor. I was too upset about the slashed portrait to register the connection at the time."

"Crystal was a mass of sequins at the party," interjected Marianne. "You think she left the party and went into your studio and slashed her mother's portrait?"

"I believe so," said Ami. "That was a spiteful and childish act."

"Spiteful fits her psychological profile," agreed Marianne. "The sequins will prove Crystal was there.

That's opportunity. And her motive was to get rid of Julie so she could have Jerry."

"Before the police came that night, I looked closely at the area from my studio to Julie's body. There was a crushed cigarette butt nearby. Julie didn't smoke."

"Crystal could have left the cigarette butt," said Marianne. "Did you notice any sequins?"

"No, I didn't notice any, but that doesn't mean the police didn't find one or two in that area."

"The party was a no smoking zone so that's no help in guessing the smoker. Have you noticed anyone smoking since you've been here?" asked Marianne.

"Not that I can recall. Unfortunately, we don't know this community," said Ami. "We have no in-roads with the neighbors here, so it's going to be harder for us to get information."

"We know Bill and he seems to know everyone's secrets," said Marianne. "I have no hesitation pumping him for information. I think he'd enjoy it and be happy to help!"

"Before we approach Bill, we need to do some ground work right here. As soon as I'm finished breakfast, let's thoroughly examine the area where you found Julie."

>=<

Ami examined the ground around the police tape. "I'm sure she was killed here. Not killed somewhere else and dumped here."

"You mean because there are no drag marks? It's pretty rocky though. They may not show up."

"No, because of all these blood splatters. I'm assuming either the police have the weapon or the killer took it away with them. And the cigarette butt is gone so I'm assuming the police have it. My guess is Crystal

58

stabbed her with the same knife she used to slash the portrait."

"I remember that when I bent over Julie's body, her chest was covered in blood. She must have been stabbed a number of times. How horrible!"

"I'm sorry, Dear. You don't have to talk about if it upsets you."

"No. It's healing to talk about it. And the more details I can remember, the more it will help us."

"Hello," greeted Chief Dawson from the top of the stairs. "I hope you're not disturbing my crime scene."

"No. We were very careful not to use the stairs. We used the side path," answered Marianne.

"What are you doing?" he asked.

"Trying to rid myself of the emotional trauma of finding Julie," said Marianne. "We thought if I came down and relived it, it would help."

"Did it?"

"I think so. I recalled how the blood covered her chest and how it looked like someone had stabbed her a number of times," she said, honestly.

"That's pretty gruesome recall," he commented.

"I think that's enough, Marianne. Let's go," suggested Ami. "I'm sure Chief Dawson has work to do."

They turned and started up the side path to the house.

Chief Dawson joined them as they neared the top. "I had an interesting talk with Captain Andrews at Seashell Beach. He sends his regards, by the way. Mrs. Dautry, I hope you and your niece aren't amateur investigating."

Marianne took an intake of breath.

Ami looked up at him. "I assure you, Chief Dawson, if, by any chance, anything remotely related to this murder crosses my path, I will notify you immediately."

"I'm reassured to hear that." He stepped aside.

Ami and Marianne continued up the path and into the house.

"Are we going to see Bill now?" asked Marianne once they were inside.

"Yes," answered Ami.

>=<

After giving Marianne and Ami a guided tour of his garden, Bill led them to a secluded seating area. His staff brought a tray of sandwiches, cakes and lemonade and set it on the table. "Please, help yourselves. Now, what can I tell you?"

"We want dirt on the closest people in Julie's life," said Marianne. She picked up a sandwich and bit into it. "Ooh, this is scrumptious! What is it?"

Bill smiled at her. "Roasted lamb and cucumber with cilantro dressing. One of my favorites. I'm so happy you like it, mon très cher."

"I love it! Now, tell us the dirt."

"Dirt on close people, huh? Well, besides Meg, the three closest people in Julie's life were number one, crazy Crystal. You've seen her in action. Number two, joyless Jerry. Julie's priority was Crystal, not him. As Meg mentioned, he finally had enough and called it quits the day of the party. Number three was avatar Arthur. Julie sought his advice and counsel during emotional upheavals with Jerry or Crystal."

"Is Crystal why Arthur left Julie for Sharon?" asked Marianne.

"It was Julie who left Arthur for Jerry. As I mentioned at the party, Julie had needs that Jerry was eager to meet. Sharon was happy to mend Arthur's broken heart, which I doubt was broken. I think Arthur was relieved to be free of Julie and Crystal. And I think he truly loves Sharon. She is a much better match for him."

"What about Sharon?" asked Marianne. "Seems to me she'd be suspicious of Julie running to Arthur all the time for comfort."

"Julie often ran to Sharon for comfort as well. She considered her a close friend. Sharon doesn't appear the jealous type. Although if you want to include her, then, suspicious Sharon would make four."

"What about the theater guild?" asked Ami. "Meg said something about Julie wanting to expel a few of the members."

"Oh, yes, that," said Bill. He took a sip of lemonade. "We have a handful of members who like the status but not the work. Julie wanted them off the board. She had Karen Hastings siding with her on her ousting efforts. Karen oversees the theatrical production business end. Amazingly competent and formidable. Between the two of them, those deadwood board members didn't stand a chance. I think Alex Sutton was the only member who cared enough to fight Julie about it. Being a board member meant a lot to him. He's a local artist. Used to be very active with designing, organizing and helping paint scenery. A couple of years ago, he had some health issues and couldn't participate much. Over this past year, he regained this health, but we haven't regained his participation. He was particularly vocal about fighting Julie if she tried to remove him."

"What about business associates?" asked Ami.

"Business owners in this community make an effort to get along. Julie had no business competitors here. She had total control of her business. No partners. One part time employee, Gina Southerland, retired school teacher. A real gem. Efficient. Personable. They got on happily. I doubt she would remain, even if the shop managed to stay in business, which it won't without Julie."

"Can you think of anyone else who might have had a reason to want Julie dead?"

"As far as I know, the only real enemy Julie ever had was her ex-husband. They had a very nasty divorce when Crystal was a child. He moved to Oregon. No further contact. Didn't even bother to keep in touch with his little daughter. Not only has he been out of the picture for years, but he died of cancer several months ago. Surprisingly, he left Crystal a little money. Not much. Less than twenty thousand, I think. Julie put it in Crystal's account. Clearly, he didn't kill her. Crystal remains my chief suspect."

"Aunt Ami thinks so, too," informed Marianne. "And she can prove Crystal is the one who slashed the portrait."

"Well, that makes sense," agreed Bill. "Tell me about the proof."

"I noticed sequins, similar to those on Crystal's dress, on the floor of my studio. And the canvas was cut right to left. That would most likely mean a left-handed person. I noticed Crystal held that threatening cheese knife in her left hand. Also, slashing is a spiteful act, which would fit Crystal's personality."

"Whoever killed Julie was angry. She was stabbed in the chest repeatedly. I noticed her chest was covered in blood when I found her," informed Marianne.

"The repetition was, most likely, caused by anger, but it could have been by necessity, if the killer wasn't strong, to ensure she didn't survive," suggested Ami.

"Also, Aunt Ami noticed a crushed cigarette butt not far from Julie's body. The police took it away. It could have been the killer's. Do you know if Crystal smoked? If not, who at the party smoked?"

Bill sat back and stared at them. "You amaze me. My initial assessment of you, Ami, was creative, intelligent and independent. I regarded you, Marianne, as youthfully outspoken, clever and fun. At that time, I hadn't encountered your ninja aspect." He winked at her. "Now, I'm shocked by your interest in this murder, your outlining of clues, your discussion of blood with no aversion to the gore. I'm stunned," admitted Bill.

"I'm sorry we've shocked you," said Ami. "We didn't want to waste time being evasive."

"Have we totally turned you off or are you still willing to help us?" asked Marianne.

"You haven't turned me off. If anything, I am more fascinated with you than ever. And, yes, I will happily help you, mon très cher."

>=<

"Would you happen to have a cup of coffee?" asked Chief Dawson when Marianne answered his knock on the French door.

"Sure. Come on in," she answered. "Or would you rather sit on the deck?"

"Deck's fine," he said, walking over to a chair.

"I'll bring it right out."

"Can you bring your aunt with you? I'd like to talk with both of you."

Marianne gulped. "Sure," she said.

A moment later, Ami opened the door and joined Chief Dawson. Marianne followed with a tray of coffee mugs.

Ami handed Chief Dawson a mug. "What do you want to talk about?" she asked.

"I had an interesting conversation with Josh. He said you had a productive visit with Bill where you assessed clues and motives and reviewed suspects. Just wondered if you'd like to share anything with me."

"That snitch!" accused Marianne.

Ami gave her niece a silencing stare. "Of course, we discussed Julie's murder with Bill. Why wouldn't we?

It's foremost on all our minds. We're all concerned as to who killed Julie."

"We think it was Crystal," said Marianne.

"I see. The winner in your game of 'who done it' was Crystal."

"I don't consider this a game," said Ami. "A woman lost her life. It happened on my door step. I take that very personally. I'm sad that her life was cut short. And I'm sad for those who loved her."

He raised his eyebrow. "Well said. I appreciate your sincerity."

"Although," said Marianne, "Aunt Ami has proof that Crystal is the one who slashed the portrait. And she noticed a cigarette butt near Julie's body."

"Marianne, I can speak for myself."

"Well, you might not have mentioned it and I want him to know everything we know because I like him," said Marianne.

Chief Dawson let out a hearty laugh.

Ami smiled. "As you can see, she has no filter."

"Tell me about the cigarette butt?" he asked Ami.

"I noticed it that night before the police arrived. I also noticed it was gone in the morning. I don't think it's related to the crime, but I assume you know more about it than we do."

"Is it true you have proof Crystal slashed the portrait?" he asked.

"I noticed the sequins on the floor of my studio matched those on the dress Crystal wore that evening," answered Ami. "I doubt I'm telling you anything you don't already know."

"What else did you notice?" he asked.

"Just that the direction of the slashes on the painting indicate a left-handed person did it and I noticed Crystal is left handed."

"When did you notice she is left-handed?"

"When she point the cheese knife at me. She picked it up and held it in her left hand. Also, she seemed comfortable threatening me with a knife. There was a confidence level evident. As if she had experience using a knife as a weapon."

Chief Dawson stared with admiration at Ami. "I find you an intriguing woman, Mrs. Dautry."

Ami blushed and looked out at the ocean.

"What about me? Don't you find me intriguing?" asked Marianne.

He turned to Marianne. "Definitely. And since I like you," he said, nodding at her, "I'm going to share a bit of information."

"Ooh, spill," said Marianne.

"Crystal confessed to slashing the portrait. And yes, she identified the sequins as being from her dress."

"One crime solved! And, if you have the dress, you've solved Julie's murder. Wasn't it covered in blood from all those stabs?" asked Marianne.

"I can't discuss anything else," answered Chief Dawson.

"But you said you like me," countered Marianne.

"He may like you, but he only provided what I read on the local news feed this morning. It said Crystal confessed to slashing the portrait and is a person of interest in the death of her mother," interjected Ami. "I doubt they have the dress or they would have arrested her. My guess is Crystal dumped it somewhere."

"I understand how tempting it is to discuss this murder and assess suspects. It appears you trust and enjoy talking with Bill and Josh."

"Well, I don't trust Josh since he snitched on us," said Marianne.

"He was concerned about you. And so am I. The person who killed Mrs. Crestly did so brutally. He won't hesitate to kill either or both of you if you guess upon his identity."

"But Crystal killed Julie," objected Marianne.

"She has not been charged and she is currently free on bail." He turned to Ami. "She's already threatened you once.   I'd like you to promise me you won't discuss suspects with anyone else."

"Agreed," said Ami.

"Me, too," said Marianne.

CHAPTER EIGHT

The Dinner

"Well, look what was hand delivered," said Marianne walking out to the deck.

"What is it?" asked Ami.

Marianne handed her an engraved envelope.

"Expensive stationery," noted Ami, ripping it open.

"The guy who delivered it was wearing a uniform."

"What kind of uniform?"

"Like an old movie chauffeur would wear."

"You're joking!"

"Nope."

"It's an invitation to an intimate dinner at eight o'clock Saturday evening."

"Let me guess," said Marianne. "Sharon Hart Randall?"

"Yes." Ami handed Marianne the invitation.

Marianne's cell rang. She looked at the caller ID. "It's Bill," she said. "Hi Bill! Yes. We got one, too. This invitation says 'intimate.' Translate, please. I see. And describe 'cocktail attire' since I'm assuming I can't wear flip-flops. Really! Can't wait to tell Aunt Ami. Bye!"

"And those definitions to our hostess?" asked Ami.

"Intimate means no more than eight guests at the table. Cocktail attire means men wear business suits. Women wear knee-length dresses, no ostentatious gems."

"Did you remember to pack a cocktail dress?" teased Ami.

"I don't think I've ever seen one. Sounds like something from the olden days. Wait a minute, that show about the early sixties had those dresses. Did women really wear dresses and heels everywhere back then?"

"I suppose many women did," answered Ami.

"Did you?"

"No."

"Why not?"

"Because I wasn't born yet. Do the math, Dear."

"Oh, right. Then, I guess neither of us has one," replied Marianne. "Let's go shopping!"

>=<

"That rose color really flatters your skin tone," said Marianne, as Ami walked into the living room.

"And I love the blue on you," responded Ami.

"Thanks, but the fun of buying it has worn off. Now, that I'm actually wearing it, it feels weird, like a costume and I'm an actor on a stage."

"It feels weird because it's not something you would normally wear."

"I didn't mind the party where I could hide out with Bill and gossip, but this phony baloney dress-up dinner party smacks of pretense," complained Marianne. "The people living here have it all wrong. The beach is supposed to be casual attire. Somebody needs to set them straight."

"I hear a little of your mother in those comments," said Ami.

"Heaven forbid!" replied Marianne. "But you have to admit it's over-the-top."

"Over-the-top to me is how much money I've spent on dresses since I've been here. I doubt rewearing them to other events would be considered fashionably appropriate. So, I guess the choices are leaving them in the closet or donating them to charity."

"You could put them up for sale at one of those consignment stores," suggested Marianne.

"I guess I could check that out. We should get going," said Ami, opening the front door.

"The sky is bright and clear," commented Marianne. "At least, we'll start off the evening with an enjoyable five-minute walk."

"Now, that optimistic tone sounds more like Marianne."

>=<

The dinner party guests included Bill and Josh, Meg and Carl, Ami and Marianne with Sharon and Arthur sharing hosting duties.

Before entering the dining room, Sharon's personal assistant met with the guests as a group. They were given instructions to turn off their phones and not to discuss politics, religion, or anything associated with Julie's murder.

After being seated, Sharon nodded to a crisply uniformed man to begin serving the courses.

Although Marianne had been to several formal dinner parties, she'd never been assaulted by so much crystal and silverware. She eyed the other guests and followed their lead.

"Ami, I had an opportunity to review your website. You are an exceptionally talented artist. I was wondering if we could meet sometime in the next week or so to discuss your painting my portrait," suggested Sharon.

"Of course. Why don't you call me and we'll coordinate our schedules?" responded Ami.

"I congratulate you on your website," said Arthur. "It's beautifully designed."

"That's Marianne's creation. Computer graphics is her field," informed Ami.

"It seems exceptional artistic talent runs in the family. I understand you design computer games as well," said Sharon.

"Matty called her gaming royalty," interjected Meg.

"Matty Westford?" asked Arthur. "His grandfather and I play golf. Matty got him hooked on gaming and now John has me hooked."

"Arthur and his computer games," said Sharon, smiling. "He thoroughly enjoys his mindless pursuit."

"Gaming is quite the opposite of mindless," objected Marianne. "Studies have proven gaming increases gray matter in the right hippocampus, right prefrontal cortex and cerebellum which means that memory, strategy, fine motor skills and spatial navigation are all improved. And gaming is being used medically as well, to help with injury rehabilitation and to treat depression."

"I had no idea," replied Sharon. "I apologize for my thoughtless comment. Thank you for educating me, Marianne."

"I told you I wasn't wasting my time," crowed Arthur. "Thank you, Marianne, for providing me with more reasons to play."

"Oh, dear," said Sharon. "Not more reasons? I'm afraid I shall never see you." She placed her hand to her cheek in feign despair.

"I could teach you to play and we could enjoy it together," coaxed Arthur. "Matty introduced John and me to this TriangleTarget game. It started off easy, but became progressively difficult. Now, we're hooked and can't give it up." He laughed.

Marianne smiled but said nothing.

"That's an enigmatic smile, Marianne. Do you not like that that game?" asked Arthur

"I love that game," answered Marianne.

"Honey, if you don't tell him, I will," said Meg.

"I created that game, Arthur."

"How impressive," said Arthur with admiration. "It's a splendid game. I have to admit John is a much better player. Always levels up before me. Currently, he's stuck on level thirteen, so it's the first time I've caught up."

Arthur gave Marianne an embarrassed smile and coughed lightly. "If you don't mind, may I beg a favor? I'd love, just once, to get the jump on John and see him frown. I'm all for fair play and would fess up afterward. Do you think you can give me a clue?"

Marianne leaned toward Arthur. "The key to level thirteen is yellow triangle combination."

Arthur's eyes twinkled. "Thank you." He sat back and smiled broadly.

"You've made Arthur extremely happy, Marianne. That was generous of you. I can see why Bill is so taken with you."

Marianne glanced over at Bill.

He winked a response.

"Bill, I asked Georgio to prepare a cutting for you of the heirloom rose he added to my garden. The fragrance is heavy with raspberry. It's delightful. I thought you might enjoy it."

"That was thoughtful of you, Sharon. Thank you!" replied Bill.

"Josh, I understand Randall has completed the script and some of the lyrics for next year's musical. What do you think of it?"

"I think we have a winner. His script is clever. It all takes place at a party so we can use the whole stage as one room and spotlight different actors for the interactions and songs, eliminating the need for scene changes. His lyrics are humorous. I've been playing with them and they lend themselves naturally to music. I'm optimistic about the composing going smoothly."

"Has Elise agreed to play the lead again?" asked Sharon.

"You know we always hold open auditions," replied Josh.

"Yes, but Elise always wins out. Don't you think a change might be refreshing? Perhaps Ami would like to audition," offered Sharon.

"No, thank you. I love the theater, but strictly as an audience member," said Ami.

"If acting isn't your forte, I'm sure your artistic talent would be a welcomed addition to our production. We always need help painting scenery. Can we count on your participation?" asked Sharon.

"I don't want to commit at present. I'm still in the process of moving in," offered Ami.

"Josh said there won't be scene changes so there won't be anything for Aunt Ami to paint."

Sharon shot Marianne a disapproving glare.

"The play is a long way off still. We have plenty of time for discussing those details," smoothed Josh.

"Carl, I understand the new time share addition to the resort is almost complete. When can we expect occupancy?" asked Sharon.

"In the Fall," said Carl.

"How nice," answered Sharon. "I assume you'll be handling the sales end, Meg."

"Yes," Meg answered.

>=<

"You certainly impressed Arthur, Dear. Did you enjoy the evening?" asked Ami as they walked home.

"I think my favorite part of the evening was popping Sharon's uninformed balloon about gaming."

"You don't like her?"

"No!" barked Marianne. "She's an elitist snob. If this was a casual dinner, how many courses does she serve for a formal one!"

"I agree it was elaborate, but it's probably everyday dining to her."

"And that stilted dinner conversation! It was like she was reading from a cheat sheet."

"I think she was attempting to be a gracious hostess by making a point to include something of interest to each of us."

"It sounded phony. And how dare she try to pressure you into painting scenes! Did you see that disapproving look she gave me when I spoke up? I really ticked her off." Marianne smiled.

"Remember, at her party, how she pushed Josh into donating his time? That's all she was doing with me. It's probably something she does without thinking."

"Well, I didn't like it! And those stupid dinner rules!"

"I didn't mind turning off my cell. I do that on my own anyway. And I can understand how some subjects can provoke heated discussions. What surprised me was the way it was handled; her assistant meeting with us so formally," said Ami.

"It was like being told how to curtsy before meeting a queen. Well, I'm not one of her subjects and I don't like being treated like one. I'm not accepting any more of her invites," vowed Marianne.

Ami laughed. "I think you turned on her the minute she criticized gaming."

"I didn't like her imperious attitude. Particularly, the way she treated Arthur."

"You mean teasing him about gaming?"

"Oh, she was pretending to tease him, but her intention was to demiss him. She's a typical passive-aggressive personality type. Basic psychology."

"I think you're being unfairly hard on her. Her behavior might seem haughty to us because we live in very different worlds. We have to work and cook dinner and do laundry. Her normal is wearing jewels and being pampered by a full staff."

"And she pushed that wealth in our faces! She's calculating and pretentious."

"I don't agree. I think she was trying to be inclusive. Her guest list was composed of people we knew. That was an attempt to make us feel comfortable."

"She invited some of our own kind. More of us to look down on."

"She wouldn't have invited us at all if that were the case. I think she put a lot of effort into her dinner party and wanted us to enjoy it. She didn't have to go to my website or ask me about painting her portrait. That was a welcoming gesture."

"Okay, I'm happy she wants you to paint her portrait."

"Me, too. I'm a working woman who now has to buy dresses I'll only wear once."

"You should quote her triple your normal fee. You can cover tonight's dress, and donate the excess to a soup kitchen."

Ami smiled.

CHAPTER NINE

The Sitting

"You look beautiful, Sharon," said Ami. "And the setting is perfect. I think sitting on the white velvet bench with the damask of the canopy bed behind you is intimate, yet tasteful. The white evening gown adds a formal note and the blue sapphires light up your eyes. You've created the exact appearance and ambiance you stated you wanted to project."

"After our meeting, I knew immediately this was the setting I wanted for my personal birthday gift for Arthur."

"I'm sure he'll cherish it," said Ami. "Ready for photographs?"

"Yes. What would you like me to do?"

"I'll walk you through it. It will go very quickly so just follow my lead. I'd like you to relax into that pose. That's right." Ami clicked quickly and continuously as she moved around Sharon. "You're sitting naturally. You're feeling relaxed. You're feeling joyful. You're feeling beautiful. You're feeling confident. Wonderful! Now, you're thinking of Arthur and how he adores you. Your eyes tell the story of your love for him. Perfect! Now, you're feeling classically romantic. You're exuding warmth. You're approachable. You're exposing just a touch of vulnerability. Very good! Just a few more. Hold your head regally. You're a ruler. You're a queen. Good! Now, show me your strength. You're a warrior. You're feeling invincible. Hold that pose. We're done!"

"Oh, my, that was quite emotional," said Sharon, fanning her face with her hands. "May I see the photographs?"

"Of course. Let me pull them up for you." Ami downloaded the photos to her tablet and handed it to

Sharon. "I'll set up the easel and canvas while you review them." Ami rolled out a tarp, set her portable easel atop it, and stood the canvas on the easel. After mixing her paint wash, she waited for Sharon to finish reviewing the photos.

"These are excellent, Ami. Do I approve one or several?"

"Before I leave, I'll ask you to choose three favorites. One for pose, one for expression and one for overall appearance. I'll focus on those, but I'll use a combination of all of the photos in the portrait."

"Is photography the norm now for portraits?"

"My process is considered old fashioned with what's happening in portraits today. Some artists computer scan facial features and print out three dimensional pieces that they then paint. Other artists use computer programs that turn photographs, like the ones I've taken of you, into portraits in the style of Rembrandt or Renoir or Kahlo. Computer graphic artists design, print and frame without ever touching paint or a brush. There's a whole new technical world open to artists."

"Oh, I much prefer what you're doing. It feels more authentic."

"I'm glad you're comfortable with it. Would you like to get a drink or walk around before we start. This will take about thirty minutes."

"No. I'm excited to begin."

"Then, here we go!" Ami picked up her brush and painted the first stroke.

>=<

"So how did your session with Sharon, the queen of the elites, go today?" asked Marianne walking out to the deck.

"It couldn't have gone better," said Ami. "Sharon was a dream subject. She looked beautiful. Her choices in makeup, clothes, furniture and atmosphere were perfect for the impression she wanted portrayed. She was cooperative and pleasant. How was your day with Bill?"

"We chose some great accessories we think you'll like. I took photos for you. Both Bill and I think you need to create an entry into the room. You don't have a foyer and it's bad feng shui for energy to rush through the front door and into the room. Energy has to be buffered as it comes in. We found a beautiful silk screen and a slim table that we think will go great together and give the illusion of a foyer. Also, since your front door has one sidelight, we think a large plant would be great there. Bill suggested a ficus because you have plenty of room for it to grow and just the right amount of light."

"That all sounds fine to me. You and Bill accomplished a great deal. Thanks for taking this on."

"You're welcome! It was fun for both of us. Bill invited us over for dinner tonight. We're going to eat in the garden. He said it's Bill casual and not Sharon casual so I can wear whatever I want."

Amy laughed.

>=<

"I spoke with Sharon today. She raved about your professionalism and talent. She stated she loves the portrait already," informed Josh.

"I'm happy she's pleased," said Ami.

"Aunt Ami said she was a dream subject; cooperative and pleasant. Maybe it was her evil twin who had us over for that phony dinner."

"I get the impression you don't like Sharon," teased Bill.

"No. I don't."

"Could your feelings have anything to do with her gaming comment?" asked Josh.

"Oh, you have to admit she was a snob about that!" howled Marianne.

"Gaming comments aside, try not to judge Sharon too harshly. She is generous and kind and means well," said Josh.

"Keep an open mind, mon très cher," added Bill.

"Even though I don't like her, I'm glad Aunt Ami has the commission. And since you're all sold on her, I'll give her one more chance, but only one."

Josh leaned into Bill. "Remind me never to criticize gaming. I don't want to be on her bad side."

Bill laughed.

"Moving on," directed Marianne. "Aunt Ami, tell Bill what you thought of the accessory photos."

"I liked them all," said Ami. "And you're on budget, except for the screen. It's beautiful and I can see why you both chose it, but it's more than I'd like to spend."

"We can eliminate something else and keep to budget," said Bill.

"Then I leave it all in your hands. Do what you'd like with the room. I very much appreciate your taking on this project. It's above and beyond."

"I'm having a great time," said Bill. "It keeps my wits sharp and creative juices flowing to dabble now and then in the old interior design game. And Marianne is a bright and enjoyable partner."

"Thanks! Bill has taught me so much!"

"Ami, I spoke with someone else today who had positive comments about you," said Josh.

"Who was that?"

"Lucas. He was impressed by how you process and synthesize information."

"I told you he had a thing for you," suggested Marianne. "The day after you snitch on us…"

"I was concerned about you," defended Josh, interrupting.

"Anyway, afterward, he came to see us. During the conversation, Lucas told Aunt Ami that he found her intriguing. She turned bright red and looked away. I had to come to the rescue by teasing him about finding me intriguing. I think she finds him attractive and is afraid to let herself get involved."

"Marianne, I can speak for myself. And you're speaking nonsense."

"It's not nonsense. He likes you and you wouldn't have blushed if you didn't like him," insisted Marianne.

"I am a recent widow who is not interested in a relationship with anyone."

"Uncle George died two years ago. That is not recent."

"Recent can only be assessed by the bereaved. End of discussion."

CHAPTER TEN

The Meeting

"These are really creative, Matty. Your portfolio shows your passion and your talent."

"So, you really think I have talent?"

"Of course. Don't you?"

"I thought I did, but my confidence has been a little shaky since I read how hard it is to break into this field."

"Success in any field takes confidence. It's helpful to get input and to continue to learn and improve your skills, but it's important you not let mine or anyone else's opinion define you. Believe in yourself."

"Thanks. I appreciate the advice and your taking time to meet with me."

"Well, I think your ideas are fun and creative and your graphics exceptionally well done. I'm texting Justin Smithson, he's the CEO of Sense Games, asking if he'll meet with you to review your portfolio and interview you for an internship. There. Done."

"I don't know how to thank you for this. You have no idea how much this means to me."

"I know what it means. I've been there. It's almost time for dinner. I'm craving some comfort food. Are you okay with pizza or is that what you live on at college?"

"I live on Thai food at college. There's a restaurant right down the street. Pizza sounds great."

"Okay! I'll get us a bottle of wine while you check if my aunt is agreeable to pizza, too. She's out on the deck."

"Hi, Mrs. Dautry," said Matty stepping onto the deck. "Marianne wants to know if you're okay with pizza for dinner."

"Sounds fine. And Matty, you can call me Ami. Was Marianne able to help you?"

"More than I expected. She's trying to get me an interview for an internship."

"I'm happy for you. You seem to have enthusiasm for the field."

"He certainly does," said Marianne, joining them with the tray of wine and glasses. She set the tray on the table, poured Matty a glass and handed it to him.. "So, pizza with lots of vegetables and pepperoni okay for everyone?"

"Fine with me," said Matty.

"Me, too," said Ami.

"Great. I'll make the call. Be right back," said Marianne, pulling her cell out of her pocket and walking into the house.

"Besides computer design, what are your interests, Matty?" asked Ami.

"To be honest, I don't have time for much else."

"Does Crystal attend the same university as you?" asked Ami, pouring herself a glass of wine.

"No. I'm at University of San Jose, in their computer science program. Crystal goes to UC Santa Cruz. She's enrolled in their liberal arts program."

"I'm very sorry Crystal lost her mother," said Ami. "How is she handling the loss?"

"I haven't seen her since Sharon's party. I texted to check on her after hearing about Julie. Nancy, she's a mutual friend, keeps in touch. She's staying with Crystal right now to help her. She said Crystal is really shook about going to jail. "

"Do you know if Crystal still plans to sue me?" asked Marianne, rejoining them on the deck.

"Nancy didn't mention it. I doubt it though cause she's got all those charges; slashing the painting and threatening you," he looked over at Ami, "and being a suspect in her mother's death. Arthur told my grandfather Crystal's attorney is a no nonsense guy who isn't taking any crap from her. He'd probably tell her she has more pressing problems than suing you."

"That's a relief!"

"I understand she's selling her mother's house and business," said Ami.

"She will once the whole probate thing clears. Nancy said Crystal's anxious to escape their shack. She's always hated that house."

"I don't understand why she would call it a shack. I've been to their home and it's lovely," said Ami.

"Crystal wants to live in a mansion like Sharon's with a full staff she can order around. That's why she hoards money."

"So it's true she has money? Meg said Crystal was broke from buying drugs," said Marianne.

Matty laughed. "Julie believed drugs were the reason for Crystal's tantrums, and Crystal let her believe it to get more money. Crystal's a health nut. She'd never take drugs. And she has plenty of money. Has it stashed away in different banks. She even has a Swiss bank account. Money is an obsession with her."

"That explains her eagerness to sell Julie's assets. I was surprised she doesn't want Meg handling the sales. She was Julie's closest friend," said Ami.

"Crystal is still salty over what Meg did at Sharon's party."

"What'd she do?" asked Marianne.

"Julie asked Meg to leave the party and go home with her. Meg didn't want to, so Jerry stepped in. Crystal blames Meg for Jerry offering. Jerry is her other big obsession."

"If she's your girl, doesn't that bother you?" asked Marianne.

"Crystal is not my girl. She saved my butt back in grade school and we kind of bonded."

"How'd she save you?" asked Marianne.

"I was seven and a nerd who got picked on a lot. One day at school, this kid, Danny Jenkins, pinned my arms behind my back. It hurt real bad and I started crying. Crystal came over and pinned his arms behind his back. Told him if he ever touched me again she'd break both his arms. She was four years older, so she was bigger than us. After he ran away crying, she told me I'd better learn to fight because she wasn't going to rescue me again. That night, I asked my dad for karate lessons. He happily signed me up the next day. I think he knew I was getting picked on."

"So you've been hanging out ever since?"

"No. I was a little kid. We didn't have anything in common. Whenever I saw her, I'd nod. You know, to let her know I appreciated what she did for me. It wasn't until the last few years that we connected. Crystal doesn't have many friends other than me and Nancy. She's selfish and controlling. Kind of hard to be around."

"Then, why do you hang out with her?" asked Marianne.

"I don't. The only time I see her is at local parties. Crystal hangs around me when she isn't with a date, which lately is always because of her obsession with Jerry. She wants to marry him. Mostly, because of his inheritance. It doesn't hurt that he's attractive."

"But Bill said Jerry made it clear he loves Julie," said Marianne.

"Crystal doesn't care. Nothing he says or does will stop her. She wants him and she'll continue to pursue him. She won't give up."

"Wow! She must have been furious when Jerry took Julie home," said Marianne.

"Oh, he didn't. They never left the parking lot. Well, not together."

"How come?"

"As soon as Jerry left the party, Crystal followed him. I followed Crystal in case she got in trouble with one of her tantrums. I kind of watch out for her. You know, pay back. I've had to help remove her and take her home on more than one occasion."

"I've heard several people reference her tantrums. Exactly what does she do?" asked Ami.

"Acts like a toddler. For instance, last month, at my grandparents' party, Jerry was dancing with Julie. Crystal ran over to them. Pushed them apart. Threw some pretty nasty words at Jerry. And even nastier ones at her mother. It was embarrassing to watch."

"And Julie let her get away with that behavior?" asked Ami.

"Julie was afraid of Crystal. My grandmother wasn't having it. She took Crystal by the arm and escorted her out of the room. I followed them cause I knew I'd have to drive her home."

"Crystal has serious psychological problems," diagnosed Marianne. "She needs therapy."

"Julie tried a few times to get her counseling, but Crystal wouldn't cooperate."

"You were telling us that at Sharon's party, Crystal followed Jerry outside and stopped him from taking Julie home," recalled Marianne.

"Yep. Spewed some pretty nasty stuff at them that night, too. Jerry got in his car and drove off. Julie ran down to the beach. Crystal saw me watching her and came back to the party."

"So Jerry drove away and Julie went to the beach alone?" asked Ami.

"As far as I know."

"I remember Crystal interrupting our conversation that night, wanting you to take her home. That's why I thought you were a couple," said Marianne.

"I'm sorry she was rude to you. I was afraid if I didn't go with her, she would throw another tantrum and I didn't want to expose you to that."

"Then, it's a good thing you drove her home when she asked," said Marianne.

"Oh, I didn't drive Crystal home."

"You didn't? Why not?"

"When we got to my car, I told Crystal I didn't appreciate her ordering me around and not to do it again. She called me a, well, an offensive slur, and jumped out of the car before I even started it."

"Where did she go?" asked Marianne.

"No idea. Didn't care either. By then, I was happy to be rid of her."

CHAPTER ELEVEN

The Lunch

"Hello, Ami. This is Elise Foster, your long absent neighbor. Lou gave me your number. I hope you don't mind."

"Of course, not."

"Good. Got back from Australia yesterday and heard the terrible news. I'm so sorry you endured that experience. I'm calling to invite you and your niece over for lunch today. I know it's short notice, but I'm anxious to meet you. Lou will be joining us. Will you come?"

"Yes, thank you."

"Wonderful! Let's say one o'clock? Oh, and let's keep it casual. Normal casual, not Sharon casual. I'm jet lagged and really don't feel like dressing up."

"That will be fine."

"Great. See you then. Bye!"

"Goodbye."

Ami turned to Marianne. "We have a lunch date with Elise Foster at one. You'll be happy to hear it's casual."

"Our kind of casual?" asked Marianne.

"Yes."

"Ooh, good. I'm dying to get a look at the inside of that house. I bet it's gorgeous!"

"Maybe she'll let you feng shui it," shot Ami.

"I bet she's already had it done. Those actors are a superstitious lot. Always trying to surround themselves with good vibes."

"Really?"

"Yes. One of my college roommates was a drama major. She had talismans all over the room."

>=<

"I love the elegance of your orchid plants, Elise," said Ami as they sat having lunch.

"Flowers play havoc with my allergies, but I so enjoy having them around. Bill suggested the orchid plants. They provide the beauty without the reaction."

"Your home is beautiful!" said Marianne.

"Thanks. I love it now, too. It took a series of stages to get to this point."

"What do you mean?" asked Marianne.

"Initially, I had it professionally decorated. It looked great, but didn't feel great. The atmosphere, the aura of the rooms, was off. I had a feng shui expert come in. That helped, but it still wasn't comfortable."

Marianne glanced with glee at Ami.

Ami gave her a keep-quiet stare.

"I get it," said Marianne. "It just didn't feel like you."

"Exactly," agreed Elise. "I tried playing with it myself. The atmosphere improved, but the look was wrong. Finally, I called Bill and begged his help. He came over and, within a few hours, we had a plan. His people came in and completed all of what you see within a week."

"Bill made excellent suggestions to Aunt Ami, too. The house is coming together beautifully."

"Do you like the house, Ami?" asked Elise.

"Very much so. Meg told me you remodeled it for your daughter. Are you comfortable with my being there?"

"Totally. I've never seen my daughter as happy as she is in Australia. So it all worked out for the best. And I'm thrilled the yoga studio works as an art studio for you."

"It's perfect," said Ami.

"Except for Crystal breaking in and slashing Aunt Ami's portrait of Julie."

"I heard about that. I'm sorry. As an artist, I know how personal our work is to us. I also heard she threatened you with a knife." She turned to Marianne. "And that you knocked her out with martial arts. Impressive!"

"You've heard a lot for being home such a short time," commented Ami.

"I filled Elise in on much of it, and we have a very vocal rumor mill. Julie's murder and the aftermath is all anyone can talk about," informed Lou.

"I just can't believe Crystal killed Julie," sighed Elise.

"The police haven't charged her," noted Ami.

"Oh, I'm sure they will," declared Lou. "Crystal had a volatile relationship with her mother. Julie got along with everyone else."

"Really, Lou?" questioned Elise.

"Oh, I know Julie could be bossy, but she didn't have enemies. If Crystal was angry enough to slash the portrait, it makes sense that she killed her mother," surmised Lou.

"I wish I had installed that surveillance system on your house," murmured Elise.

"What was that?" asked Marianne.

"I was just regretting something. I had planned to install a surveillance system on your house like I have on mine, but my security guy said my system could take in five hundred yards so it wasn't necessary."

"You have a security system with a five-hundred-yard radius?" asked Marianne.

"Yes."

"Aunt Ami's house is only two hundred yards away. Your system probably recorded the murder. You need to let the police know right away."

Elise's face went pale. "Lou, please call the police for us."

"Certainly," he rose from the table, pulled out his cell phone and walked out of the room.

"Are you all right?" asked Ami.

"When I came home, hearing that Julie was killed was terrible news, but, now, thinking about her murder actually being recorded as it happened, makes it vile and frightening. I don't want to see that video. I don't have to see it, do I?"

"Your security person will work with the police. You won't need to be involved," informed Marianne.

"Would you like us to leave so you can rest?" asked Ami.

"No! Please stay. It's comforting having you with me. Suddenly, I'm feeling vulnerable."

Ami reached out and patted Elise's hand.

"Oh my, what about the two of you? Are you safe over there all alone?" asked Elise, "I don't think I could bear having you killed, too. Why don't you come and stay here with me? I can call in extra security. It would be like Fort Knox."

"That is very kind of you, Elise, but we're perfectly safe. The police are watching Crystal. She isn't going to hurt us," assured Ami.

"Lucas is on his way," announced Lou, reentering the room.

CHAPTER TWELVE

The Threat

"Crystal, why have you come to see me?" asked Sharon as she entered the study.

"I want two million dollars."

"That's a specific amount."

"If you don't give me the money, I'm going to tell the police what you did."

"What did I do that the police would be interested in knowing?"

"I saw you that night. On the beach. Fighting with my mother."

"You must have been hallucinating. Your mother and I have never fought on the beach or anywhere else."

"Yes, you did! It was right below your stairs. The night of the party. I saw her pull her arm away from you and run down the beach."

"You are mistaken."

"No, I'm not!   Give me the money or I go to the police."

"You are an impudent girl. I understand that recently you have approached several residents in our community for money. Perhaps you've threatened them similarly. I'd like to give you a bit of advice. Threatening people is never safe. Some of them have secrets. When you threaten them, they become worried that their secrets will be exposed. Your behavior is dangerous. For your own sake, stop this foolishness before it's too late. Now, this meeting is over. You may tell the police anything you like."

"So you're not going to give me the money?"

"No, Crystal, I am not going to give you money."

"I hate you!" yelled Crystal. She deliberately smacked a vase of roses off the table and onto the floor before running out the door.

>=<

"Ami, I'm quite impressed. It is evolving beautifully," complimented Sharon. "I love the detail in the necklace. Arthur will, too."

"I knew the necklace was important to the portrait since Arthur gave it to you and wanted to accent it. It's a bit of a balancing act to get enough detail to read the sapphires but not so much as to take the spotlight from your face."

"You've certainly accomplished that. I have no changes. Please proceed to the finish."

"I'm pleased you like it," said Ami. "As I mentioned previously, when I'm through, we'll have a final brief review focused on facial subtleties. The paint will be wet so I'd like to meet again here at the studio, if possible."

"That will be fine," agreed Sharon.

"Let's go up on the deck. Marianne has prepared some lemonade for us," suggested Ami.

As they left the studio, they encountered Chief Dawson approaching.

"Chief Dawson?"

"Hello, Mrs. Dautry, Mrs. Randall. May I speak with both of you?"

"Certainly," answered Ami. "We were just going up to the deck. Please join us."

They climbed the stairs together.

Marianne was standing on the deck to greet them. "He's already questioned me. I think I have a good enough alibi," she said, looking at Chief Dawson.

He frowned at her.

"I won't say anything more," she promised.

Ami and Sharon seated themselves at the table.

Marianne poured everyone a glass of lemonade and sat down.

"Chief Dawson, what is it?" asked Ami.

"Crystal Crestly was found dead last night."

"Oh, no! I tried to warn her." Tears filled Sharon's eyes.

"What's that mean?" asked Marianne.

Chief Dawson glared at her.

"Okay. I'll let you do it," she said.

"Thank you," he answered. "Please explain, Mrs. Randall."

"She came to my house yesterday afternoon demanding two million dollars. She threatened to go to the police and tell them she saw Julie fighting with me the night of my party. It was absurd. There was no fight. She totally misunderstood our interaction."

"What was the correct interpretation of your interaction?" he asked.

"I was changing into my final fashion of the evening and movement on the beach caught my eye. From my window, I saw Julie crying. I slipped on my dressing gown and went down the outside stairs. She was distraught over a recent argument with Crystal. I explained I needed to dress and return to the party and suggested she come upstairs with me where we could talk while I dressed. I took her arm in an effort to persuade her. She expressed a need to be alone, pulled away and ran down the beach. I believe that is the interaction Crystal saw, and misinterpreted our parting."

"Thank you. What did you mean when you said you tried to warn Crystal?" asked Chief Dawson.

"Since her mother's death, Crystal has visited other members of the community, demanding money. Yesterday, when she visited me, I warned her that making threats was foolish and dangerous. Someone might think she knew something about them and panic. She was not interested in hearing what I had to say. Her focus was money."

"I'm assuming you refused. Correct?"

"Correct."

"And her response to your refusal?"

"Typically childish. She expressed her hatred for me, smashed a vase full of roses to the floor and ran out the door. I wish she had listened."

"Even if she had listened, your warning may have come too late. It's possible that the person who killed her had been threatened prior to her visiting you," noted Ami.

"What makes you assume she was killed?" asked Chief Dawson.

"If Crystal had died any other way, you wouldn't be here questioning us," answered Ami.

Chief Dawson nodded.

"Marianne mentioned giving you an alibi. I'm assuming you want one from me as well," said Ami.

"And me," said Sharon. "What time frame do you need, Lucas?"

"Between six and eleven."

"I spent the evening with Arthur, John and Elizabeth," said Sharon. "We met at six for cocktails. Followed by dinner at the club around seven. We returned to my house just after nine and played bridge until ten-thirty. John was tired so they left early. Arthur spent the night at my house."

"Thank you, Mrs. Randall."

"May I leave now, Lucas?" asked Sharon.

"Yes," he replied.

Ami escorted Sharon out.

As soon as they had left, Marianne turned to Chief Dawson. "I can't believe someone killed Crystal. She was my main suspect. Of course, just because someone killed her doesn't mean she didn't kill her mother. Logic supports her doing it. She had opportunity and motive.

Have you reviewed the surveillance tape yet? Does it confirm it was Crystal?" she asked.

"Has anyone ever mentioned that you have a tendency to be loquacious?"

"On pretty much a regular basis," she answered.

He laughed.

"What's so funny?" asked Ami, rejoining them.

"Your niece," answered Chief Dawson.

"I thought Crystal's death messed up my theory, but it doesn't," said Marianne.

"Crystal's death is a tragedy," said Ami. "She had barely begun to live life and now it's over. I feel sorry for her."

"I don't. She killed her mother. Now, go ahead and give him your alibi, Aunt Ami."

"I doubt Chief Dawson appreciates your interfering in his process, Marianne."

"It's an occupational hazard," he said. "Please tell me your movements between six and eleven last night, Mrs. Dautry."

"I expect it's similar to Marianne's since we were together during that time frame," said Ami. "Matty Westford was with us from six until midnight. After dinner, Matty and Marianne were here on the deck playing one of the games he designed. I sat with them until a little after nine. Then I sat on the deck by my bedroom and read. Matty left around midnight. It would not have been possible for any one of us to have left the house, drove to wherever Crystal was, killed her and driven back without the others noticing our being missing."

"Thank you, Mrs. Dautry."

"I wonder who she left all her money to. Probably no one. Someone that young usually doesn't have a will. How much do you think she had in that Swiss bank account of hers? Where does the money go if she didn't have a will?" asked Marianne.

Chief Dawson leaned back in his chair and took a sip of lemonade. "Where did you hear about money and Swiss bank accounts?"

"From Matty," answered Marianne. "He said Crystal was obsessed with money and had bank accounts at a number of banks and even a Swiss bank account. Don't you need like a million bucks to open a Swiss account?"

"Sometimes for private banks, but you can maintain an account in a common Swiss bank for around ten thousand dollars," informed Chief Dawson.

"How do you know that off the top of your head? You've already checked this out, haven't you? Or maybe you have a Swiss account of your own! Ooh, you're more interesting than I thought," said Marianne.

He shook his head and smiled. "I can't understand why I don't find you annoying when you clearly are."

"It's because I'm innocently annoying. It's a technique I've developed over years and years of annoying people."

"Well, you've perfected it."

"Thank you!"

"Are you two finished playing?" asked Ami with impatience.

"We are," answered Chief Dawson. "Do you have a question?"

"I have a number of them. However, I doubt you will answer any of them," stated Ami.

"Try me," he said.

"You said Crystal was found dead between six and eleven last night. How do you know the time frame? Where was she found? What was the cause of death?"

"I can tell you what's been officially released. We know the time frame because one of her friends was staying with her."

"Nancy?" asked Marianne.

Chief Dawson lifted an eyebrow.

"Easy guess. Matty told us Nancy was Crystal's only friend," answered Marianne.

"Yes, her name was Nancy. She left Crystal's house at six. When she returned with her date at eleven, they found Crystal. Medical examiner confirmed respiratory failure due to a drug overdose."

"But Matty said Crystal didn't take drugs," said Marianne. "What was the drug?" asked Marianne.

"I will not answer that. And why would you want to know?"

"It doesn't matter what the drug was," interjected Ami. "If Crystal had taken it willingly, this would not be a murder investigation."

Chief Dawson locked eyes with her. "Do you have a theory you would like to share?"

"Just observations and logic."

"You have my attention. Please continue."

"I believe Matty knew Crystal's temperament and personality well. I think he'd know if she was on drugs and he insisted she wasn't, so I accept that as truth. I think many people heard what Meg and Bill told us about Julie being concerned Crystal was buying drugs. I think Crystal was murdered and the killer used the rumor as a handy method. It would be easy to slip a drug into a drink. Crystal's death would be dismissed as an overdose and no one would recognize it as murder."

Chief Dawson's eyes twinkled. "You have a sharp mind, Mrs. Dautry."

"So, it's true? She was drugged?" asked Marianne.

"I won't answer that."

"Which brings us back to why Crystal was murdered," continued Ami. "Sharon suggested today that it was someone Crystal threatened for money. That may be true, but I don't think anyone was threatened by Crystal's accusations involving them in Julie's murder. I think the surveillance tape will confirm Crystal killed Julie so no one had a need to feel threatened."

"Of course, she killed her. She was filled with suppressed rage. Basic psychology," diagnosed Marianne.

"Her rage was hardly suppressed," stated Ami. "It was public and uncontained. There were a number of witnesses to her tantrums. I don't think she planned to kill Julie. I think on the night of Sharon's party her rage escalated when she saw Jerry and Julie leaving together. Her tantrum in the parking lot grew into slashing the portrait. It's easy to imagine that as Crystal leaves my studio, she sees Julie on the beach and while still enraged and still holding the knife, runs down the stairs and stabs her."

"I think you're right, Aunt Ami!"

"Our focus now is to find out why and who killed Crystal," said Ami. "I think we need to start with a list of the people Crystal approached for money. Sharon is correct that threatening people was dangerous. Crystal may have approached someone with a secret they did not want exposed. She, unknowingly, scared them. It's possible they went to visit Crystal last night. I can't picture Crystal as a gracious hostess, inviting someone in for a drink. She only would have invited someone in if she thought she was going to get something from them."

"Although, Mrs. Dautry, I admire your powers of deduction, and enjoy bantering with you, Mrs. Eckhart, I'd like to emphasize that there is no 'we' in my investigation. Neither of you is on my force. Neither of you has any authority to investigate. And, most importantly, neither of you is safe if you try to do so. Do you want to end up like Julie and Crystal?"

"Of course, not," said Ami.

"Then, please, stay out of this. I would be very unhappy if anything happened to you."

"Does this mean you think of us as friends?" asked Marianne.

Chief Dawson rose from his chair. "Good afternoon, ladies. Thank you for your cooperation today." He walked around the deck to the side of the house and out the front walkway.

"He thinks of us as friends," said Marianne.

>=<

"Ami, thank you for having us over for dinner tonight," said Josh, opening the wine and pouring it into the glasses.

"It's my pleasure. You've been so generous and kind entertaining us, it definitely was my turn to host."

Bill and Marianne finished grilling the steaks and brought them to the table.

"Those smell and look wonderful," said Ami.

Bill served the steaks while Marianne passed the side dishes, family style.

"I understand Lucas came over for statements regarding Crystal's death," said Bill. "He took them from us as well."

"Yes," answered Marianne. "We were with Matty last night so we alibied one another. Sharon was here approving her portrait so he took one from her, too. Did you know that Crystal tried to blackmail Sharon for two million dollars?"

"I did not know that. My rumor mill must have a glitch," said Bill. "Tell me all."

"Crystal threatened to inform the police Sharon fought with Julie the night of the murder if Sharon didn't give her the money."

"I'm assuming Sharon refused," said Josh.

"Yes," said Marianne. "Crystal got so mad she knocked over a vase of roses on her way out."

"Typically childish," commented Bill.

"Sharon said Crystal asked other people for money, too. Did she ask you?"

"No," answered Bill. "That foolish she wasn't."

"Matty said Crystal was obsessed with money and had lots of bank accounts, even a Swiss bank account," continued Marianne.

"That's a very different financial report from what Julie told Meg. And what about the drugs?" asked Bill

"Matty said Crystal didn't take drugs and lied to her mother about being broke to get more money to hide in her bank accounts."

"If she wasn't buying drugs, why did Crystal need so much money?" asked Josh.

"Matty said she was hoarding the money so she could buy a mansion and have servants."

"Well, all of this is news to me. I'm going to have to reassess my information sources," said Bill.

"If you want news about young people, you have to include them in your sources," informed Marianne. "I'll get dessert. Aunt Ami made her famous apple cake."

"Well, I guess she told you, old man," said Josh.

"She did that. Although, she had a point. I do need to include youth input," acknowledged Bill.

"I want to discuss what may be a delicate subject," said Josh as Marianne placed the tray with slices of cake on the table. "Lucas is worried you are engaging in amateur sleuthing."

"I know," said Marianne. "He said he'd be very unhappy if anything happened to us. I asked if that meant we were friends, and he left without answering."

"Whether Lucas is your friend or not, we are," emphasized Josh. "Please, I beg of you, take his and our warnings seriously. Don't poke around in this. I don't want anything to happen to you."

"All we have done is sit here on the deck reviewing scenarios with the police chief and discussing events with Bill shortly after it happened. I'd hardly call that sleuthing. We aren't roaming the neighborhood for clues or questioning people. There's no reason for concern," said Ami.

Just then the doorbell rang.

Marianne left the table to answer it and returned with Elise and Lou.

"Sorry to barge in," said Elise. "But I wanted you to know my tech guy said the tape confirms what we all thought. Crystal killed Julie. The police have it."

"Well, why didn't Chief Dawson admit that today? I asked him straight out!" said Marianne.

"My guess is he considers it police business. Please, Elise, Lou, sit and have a drink and dessert with us," invited Ami.

"Thanks," said Elise joining them at the table.

Josh poured them wine, while Marianne sliced the cake.

Elise took a sip of wine. "I thought this would be over once they had Crystal on that tape, but today I find out Crystal is dead. I'm considering going back to Australia until all of this is over. Ami, will you be okay here alone? I understand Marianne is leaving tomorrow."

"I'm staying another week or two to finish the interior design. The murders put us behind schedule."

"We're perfectly safe," assured Ami. "None of these murders have anything to do with us."

"I agree with Amy," said Lou. "The tape confirms Crystal killed Julie. And Crystal died from an overdose. It's over. We're all safe now." He took a bite of cake. "This is delicious."

"Aunt Ami made it," said Marianne.

Lou and Ami exchanged smiles.

“And it’s not over. Crystal was murdered,” said Marianne.

“Really! But we heard she died of a mix of drugs and alcohol,” said Lou.

“She did, but it wasn’t voluntary. She was drugged to make it look like an overdose,” informed Marianne.

“But why?” questioned Elise.

“The most obvious reason is what she tried with Sharon. Crystal was blackmailing people about Julie’s death,” suggested Josh. “Did she contact either of you?”

“I was told Crystal stopped by my house a couple days ago. I was out and didn’t see her. Is it possible she planned to blackmail me?” asked Elise.

“Possibly, but it doesn’t make sense to threaten you since you weren’t here when Julie was killed,” said Lou. “She didn’t contact me, unless she stopped by when I wasn’t home.”

“What if she planned to blackmail Elise about something unrelated to Julie’s death? Do you have any deep secrets, Elise?” teased Bill.

“Hardly. The tabloids have scoured my past and outed me very thoroughly over the years,” complained Elise.

“I think Bill’s suggestion that the blackmail is about something other than Julie’s death is the logical conclusion,” said Ami. “The surveillance video proves that Crystal is the one who killed Julie. So, any threats she made involving people in Julie’s death were empty. None of the people Crystal approached for money would have felt threatened by that. They knew they didn’t kill Julie.”

“So, you’re saying she threatened them about something else?” asked Josh.

“It’s more likely, they thought she knew something she didn’t,” answered Ami.

"Sharon said she had approached a number of people for money," said Marianne. "Do you have any idea who she would have approached?"

"I expect only those with a certain financial status," said Josh.

"We know she approached Sharon and tried to approach Elise. I would guess Arthur would be a target," said Lou.

"What about Matty's grandfather?" asked Marianne.

"Yes, he'd qualify," said Bill. "I wonder which one had the big secret they didn't want exposed."

"I don't know, but it must be damaging since they were willing to kill for it," said Ami.

CHAPTER THIRTEEN
The Request

"Hi Ami, I'm Jerry Robson, we met at Sharon's party and then at Julie's memorial."

"Of course, I remember. My condolences, again, on Julie's death."

"Thank you. It's been hard, but I'm dealing with it. Sorry for waylaying you in the supermarket parking lot, but I noticed you and thought I'd inquire about Julie's portrait. May I buy it?"

"Surely, you've heard that Crystal slashed it."

He gritted his teeth. "Yes. Crystal's destruction had no bounds." He offered a weak smile. "Forgive me. I'm not explaining myself very well. I spoke with Sharon recently and she raved about your portrait of her. She mentioned you work with photos. I wondered if you could paint another portrait of Julie from the photos you took of her. I'll be happy to pay whatever you want. I loved Julie. I'd like her portrait as a memory."

"I have to admit I've never painted a portrait strictly from photos. And with Julie gone, I don't know how I feel about this, Jerry. I'll need to think about it and get back to you."

"I understand it's an odd request." He handed her a card with his number. "Please, call me after you've thought it over. I hope I haven't upset you."

"Of course, you haven't. I'll need a few days to think it through, Jerry."

He nodded. "Thanks, Ami. I look forward to hearing from you."

>=<

"Ami! What a pleasant surprise!" welcomed Josh. "Bill and Marianne are out in the garden in animated conversation over your interior decor. Let's go join them."

Ami followed him to the table where Bill and Marianne were sitting reviewing accessory photos on Marianne's tablet.

"Ami! Lovely to see you," greeted Bill.

"Tea, Ami, or would you prefer something else?" asked Josh.

"Tea is fine, thanks."

Josh poured tea for both Ami and himself and then sat beside Ami.

"You have a worried brow, Aunt Ami. What's up?" asked Marianne.

"I'll tell you, but please hold your comments, Marianne. I'd like to hear from Josh and Bill first."

They all focused their attention on her.

"Jerry Robson stopped me in the supermarket parking lot and asked me to paint a portrait of Julie for him. What are your thoughts?"

Bill's mouth opened, then closed. Josh looked over at Bill before looking back at Ami.

"I take it you consider asking for a portrait of a recently murdered partner a little odd," surmised Ami.

"Yes," answered Josh. "But let's put it in context. Jerry is grieving. His request is almost certainly clouded by emotion. Julie's loss is a deep hole in his life. Perhaps he feels a portrait will fill the void."

"I agree with your reasoning, but it's still a strange request," said Bill. "Did he seem emotional?"

"No. He was controlled and polite. There was slight jaw clenching at the mention of Crystal."

"That's understandable. He could hardly view her fondly after she stabbed his love to death," said Bill.

"He admitted his request was a little odd and said he hoped he hadn't upset me."

“What did you tell him, Aunt Ami?”

“I told him I needed a few weeks to think about it. He asked me to call him and let him know.”

“Well, I don’t need any time to think about. It’s morbid. Don’t do it,” said Marianne.

“When you think about it, a request for a posthumous portrait of a loved one is not that unusual. Museums and old homes are filled with such portraits,” offered Josh.

“True, but how many were requested shortly after the loved one was murdered?” asked Bill.

“None! It’s weird!” emphasized Marianne.

“I agree with Josh that this is probably an emotional request. Jerry, more than likely, will change his mind as he processes his grief,” suggested Ami. “I waited a year before making important decisions after George died, just to be sure of clear judgment.”

“What if he doesn’t change his mind? Do you think you would paint the portrait?” asked Bill.

“No,” answered Ami.

“That was firm,” said Bill.

“I know. I’m surprised myself. Seems I don’t need time to think about it.”

“What do you think changed your mind?” asked Josh.

“Sadness,” said Ami. “As we were discussing this, I felt this overwhelming sadness for Julie. Painting Julie now would feel too sad. I couldn’t do it. Not even to honor her memory.”

“I feel sad for her, too,” said Josh. “I keep imagining the heartbreak she must have felt having the daughter she’d pampered all her life kill her so violently. Can you imagine her thoughts during her final moments? It’s tragic on every level.”

"So deeply disheartening," agreed Bill. "The feeling of betrayal and the physical and emotional pain as death takes over? Oh, it breaks my heart."

"Please, please, please stop," begged Marianne. "I can't hear any more. If the three of you continue, I'm going to cry. It's too depressing. Do you think you can change topics?"

"Of course, mon très cher," said Bill.

"I suppose I did take us down a gruesome path," said Josh. "Sorry."

"I think I was the worst," confessed Bill.

"I started it," admitted Ami.

"Let's agree you all equally contributed. Now, can we please talk about something else?"

"Why don't you tell Ami about the feng shui plans for her interior?" suggested Bill.

"Yes, I'd like to hear about that," said Ami.

"Bill and I need to take over your house next Tuesday to complete the interior design. Is that okay?"

"That depends on what you expect of me," answered Ami.

"Only that you stay out of our way. You can visit someone or hide away in your studio or go shopping. We just need full access from nine to five."

"No problem. I'll work on Sharon's portrait in my studio and arrange a lunch date with Meg. That should keep me out of your way for awhile."

"And should you need a further hide-a-way, you are welcome to lounge here in the garden," offered Josh.

"That's kind of you, Josh. Thank you," said Ami.

"Great idea, Josh," said Marianne. "Aunt Ami should come here after her lunch date and not come to the house until Bill or I call. That way, we'll have everything in place for the reveal."

"The reveal. I like your showmanship!" said Bill.

"Hi, Marianne!"

"Hi, Matty! What's up?"

"Just wanted to stop by and give you this as a thank you." He handed Marianne a bottle of wine. "Justin Smithson agreed to interview me! It's next week. It wouldn't have happened without you. I appreciate it."

"My pleasure. You're creative and talented. I'm sure your interview will go well. Do you want to come in?"

"Thanks, but I can't. Meg's arranged a private memorial for Crystal later this morning and she's asked me to speak. I need to figure out what I'm going to say."

"Oh, I didn't know one had been planned."

"It's really private, just me and Nancy, Sharon and Arthur and Meg and Carl. Meg wanted to keep all the gawkers away. You know, because of the murders. If you want to come, I can ask Meg."

"Thanks, but I don't think it would be appropriate for me to attend. I didn't know Crystal. Meg is right to keep it private."

"Well, thanks again for getting me the interview."

"You're welcome, Matty. Bye!"

"Hello, Marianne, is Ami available?" asked Lucas when Marianne answered the door.

"Someone else hasn't been murdered, have they?" she asked.

"No. I'm here unofficially," answered Lucas.

"She's out on the deck. Come on in."

Lucas followed Marianne to the deck.

"Hi, Ami," greeted Lucas. "No cause for alarm. I'm here unofficially."

"That's a relief. Please have a seat. Would you like some lemonade?" asked Ami, pointing to the pitcher on the table.

"No, thanks. I just stopped by for a moment. I have a couple of tickets to an art show downtown next Friday night. It's featuring young portrait artists from nearby colleges. I thought it might interest you. Would you like to join me?"

Marianne turned and walked into the house providing her aunt and Lucas some privacy. She flashed a broad grin.

"The exhibit does sound interesting and I would love to attend, but as a recent widow, I'm not ready for dating."

"Then, let's not consider it a date. What if we approach this as two independent portrait enthusiasts attending an art exhibit together? No expectations. Would that be agreeable?"

"Under those conditions, I'd like to join you," agreed Ami.

"Great. I'll stop by for you at eight." He took the pathway from the deck to the front rather than going back through the house.

Marianne walked onto the deck as soon as Lucas left. "So? Are you going?"

"Before you start, it's definitely not a date. We are simply two portrait enthusiasts attending an art exhibit together."

"Pllllllease! He's an enthusiast of you, not portraits."

"You don't know his art interests and I'm not discussing this any further."

"Fine. Call it whatever you want. I'm just happy you're going."

>=<

“Hello, Marianne,” greeted Sharon. “Is Ami at home?”

“She’s out on the deck. Come with me.”

Sharon followed Marianne to the deck where Ami was relaxing.

“I apologize for dropping by unannounced. I wondered if I might have a word with you.”

“Of course. Would you like to join me in a cup of tea?”

“That would be lovely,” said Sharon.

“I’ll fix it, Aunt Ami.”

“Thanks, Dear,” said Ami.

“No problem,” tossed Marianne, walking into the house.

“You and Marianne seem to have a close relationship. I imagine you’ll miss her when she goes back home.”

“Yes, I will. Even with our age difference, we’ve developed a loving friendship over the years.”

“Friends are important in life. I have many acquaintances, but few close friends. Julie was a close friend. Arthur and I attended Crystal’s memorial this morning. It reawakened my sadness over Julie.”

“I’m sorry you lost your friend. I know how painful that is.”

“Thank you.”

“Marianne mentioned Meg had arranged something private for Crystal. It was kind of her to do that.”

“Meg did it to honor Julie. She knew Julie would want her to take care of Crystal even under these circumstances.”

“I’m sure it’s been difficult for all of you,” said Ami.

“Yes, it has. It’s been a mix of sadness and anger. What Crystal did to Julie was unforgiveable, but it’s sad she died so young. I know Julie won't rest until the person who killed Crystal is held accountable. I feel an obligation to Julie to do something about it. Lucas is an intelligent investigator, but if Crystal was killed by someone she tried to blackmail, money and power will keep key information hidden from the police. And that is why I have come to you. I have a request."

"What is it?"

"I understand that in addition to your artistic talents, you have a logical and deductive mind for solving crimes. Bill has informed me that you are somewhat of a sleuth. I want to commission you to uncover Crystal's killer."

"I'm afraid Bill has misled you. I'm no detective."

"I understand, where you lived previously, you furnished the police with key information in solving a murder."

"Where did you hear that?"

"Lucas mentioned it to Josh. Bill informed me."

"I see. Well, that was different. I had lived there for years and knew that community inside out. Gathering information was simply gossiping with neighbors. I can't do that here. I'm a stranger. If I approached someone and started asking questions about Crystal, they would be suspicious. It just wouldn't work," explained Ami.

"I can assist you with inquiries. People will talk with me. I know this community intimately. You can direct me and I can obtain whatever information you need."

"I'm sure you could. It's just that I'm not sure I'd know where to begin."

"Don't be so modest," said Marianne, placing the tea tray on the table. "You've already begun. Your mind has been swirling with thoughts about Crystal's murder."

"Personal musings only. No plan of any kind," objected Ami.

"I'm leaving you two alone to enjoy your tea," said Marianne. "My parting words are for you to join forces and create a plan."

CHAPTER FOURTEEN

The Exhibit

"Hi Ami!"

"Matty! How nice to see you. Do you have a portrait in the exhibit?"

"No. I am a portrait in the exhibit. One of my friends painted me and is showing it. I'm here for moral support."

"I'd love to see it," said Ami.

"Follow me. It's to the right."

"I'll be over in a minute. I'm waiting for someone."

"Marianne?" asked Matty excitedly.

"No. She isn't with me tonight."

"Okay. See you later," said Matty cheerily, walking away.

"Champagne, okay?" asked Lucas, handing her a glass.

"Of course. Thank you. I just saw Matty. Seems a friend of his painted his portrait and is showing it. It's to the right. Want to see it?"

"Sure."

They walked through the small group and easily found the portrait of Matty.

"Are you the artist?" asked Ami of the young man standing next to it.

"Yes. I'm Scott Wilson. What do you think?" he asked, looking back and forth between Ami and Lucas and settling on Lucas.

"She's the portrait artist," said Lucas. "It's her opinion that will hold more value. I'm an art admirer only."

"I'd still like your opinion," said Scott.

"Okay, then. I like the bright color of his shirt and the way the light frames his face. I like his smile. He evokes fun. Your painting makes me want to meet him."

"I like that. Thanks!"

"I agree with Lucas," said Ami. "I like his smile, too. It holds humor and is just a little mischievous. I'm particularly impressed with what you've done with his eyes."

"Meaning?" slyly asked Scott.

"You painted eyes within his pupils and then eyes within those pupils. You have three sets of eyes in one."

Scott picked up his tablet and made a note. "So far, twelve people have stopped by and only two of you have noticed that. I'm excited you did!"

"I hadn't noticed," admitted Lucas. "But now I'm curious. What's the significance of three sets of eyes?"

"Would you like to venture a guess?" Scott asked Ami.

"As an artist, you could have any number of personal reasons, but, I'll guess you are eluding to Matty's conscious, subconscious and unconscious."

Scott smiled widely. "Yes! Please, I'd love to hear more of what you think."

"Okay. Let's discuss your technique. I like the way you built up the skin tones with semi-transparent applications. Your use of small strokes on the cheeks forms them naturally. Also, you used the tip of your brush to subtly outline the features. Your use of those techniques created prominent and pleasing facial features."

"I was attempting to copy Botticelli's technique."

"Yes, I can see that. It's very well done."

"Hi Ami! Hi Lucas!" said Matty joining them. "Do you like it?"

"I like it very much," said Ami.

"So do I," said Lucas.

"Scott's a talented artist. He just needs more exposure. His goal is his own show one day."

"Matty, I was hoping I'd see you here," said a pretty girl with dark hair, walking up to him. A nice looking young man accompanied her.

"Oh, Nancy, Paul, I want you to meet some friends of mine."

"Unfortunately, Chief Dawson and I have met a number of times. It seems Paul and I are suspects. His investigation is never ending."

"Be nice, Nancy," said Matty. "I want you to meet Ami Dautry. She's a well known portrait artist and she loves Scott's painting."

"Yes, I heard about you from Crystal," Nancy said icily.

"Come on, Nancy, all of that was Crystal's fault and you know it."

Nancy looked down at the floor and then back up at Ami and Lucas. "Sorry," said Nancy. "It's just that her death still hurts, especially since no one cares she was murdered."

"I care," said Lucas.

"It's your job to care until you arrest someone," accused Nancy.

'I care, too," said Ami. "I'm sorry for your loss."

"Thanks," she answered, and then added. "I'm usually not this rude. I'm being emotional. I shouldn't have taken my anger out on you," she said.

"I understand grief. I know what it's like to lose someone you love," said Ami.

"It's just hard hearing how much people hate her. Even though she did something horrible, she didn't deserve to be murdered."

"No, she didn't," agreed Lucas.

"I have been thinking more about the night she died," said Nancy, looking directly at Lucas. "I know the wine glasses and the drugs were on the table, and I understand someone could have slipped the drugs in her drink, but I don't believe Crystal invited anyone over. She was aware everybody hated her and she didn't want to leave the house or see anyone."

"So, you think Crystal took the drugs herself?" asked Ami.

"Of course, not. Crystal didn't take drugs," stated Nancy. "She was very particular about her diet; organic, low sugar, vegetable smoothies, lots of supplements."

"Would she have invited someone in that she trusted?" asked Ami.

"Crystal didn't trust anyone. She barely trusted me and Matty," said Nancy.

"Is it possible Crystal allowed someone in she may have approached earlier in the week?" asked Ami.

"You mean one of the people she tried to blackmail?" noted Matty.

"That's a nasty word, Matty. Besides, they all turned her down," informed Nancy.

"One of them could have had a change of mind," suggested Ami.

"I suppose, but even if she did let him in, she wouldn't have sat around having a drink with him," said Nancy. "I can't talk about this anymore."

"I'm sorry you're hurting," said Ami.

"I appreciate the information you've provided," said Lucas. "If you think of anything else, you know how to contact me."

"To be honest, I wish I could stop thinking about it. It's too sad," said Nancy. Tears trickled down her face.

Paul put his arm around her. "Let's stop talking about it and go get a drink. Okay?"

"Yes. Let's go."

Matty smiled at her.

"Your smile is just like in the painting," said Nancy. "It's a good painting," she said, walking away.

"I agree. It is a good painting. Scott, you're a talented artist," said Ami.

"Thank you."

Lucas turned to Ami. "What do you say we move along and view other paintings?"

"Yes, we should," she responded.

"Thanks for stopping by," said Scott. "And for your supportive comments."

"Let me know when you have your own show, I'd love to come," said Ami.

"Thanks! I'll make sure you get an invite!"

>=<

"So, how was your outing with Lucas? I notice you didn't invite him in for a drink," greeted Marianne.

"We viewed some very nice portraits and enjoyed talking with a number of talented young artists. There was an exceptionally nice portrait of Matty painted by his friend."

"Really! I would love to see it. Maybe Matty can text me a photo. Did you and Lucas find each other's company pleasant?"

"The focus of our conversation was on art and we both enjoyed the exhibit. We ran into Crystal's friend Nancy. Initially, she wasn't happy to see either Lucas or me. Matty acted as buffer. In the end, she admitted she feels alone in her grief for Crystal. I felt sorry for her."

"Well, she is alone. Just because Crystal's dead doesn't mean people suddenly developed affection for her. People don't like kids who kill their mothers."

"Nancy had some doubts about how the drugs got into Crystal's system. She and Matty both agreed that

Crystal didn't trust anyone and wouldn't have invited in the killer who drugged her drink."

"Obviously, they're wrong because the police found the drugs in her body," noted Marianne. "So, did you kiss Lucas goodnight?"

"Don't be ridiculous. I'm going to bed."

>=<

"Isn't it a great morning!" said Marianne walking out to the garden to join Bill. "Less than a week before our big reveal. I'm really excited!"

"I can see that," said Bill.

"Well, aren't you?"

"Yes. Although not as exuberantly as you," he responded. "Is anyone as exuberant as you?"

"No. It's my super power," said Marianne. "I know Aunt Ami is going to love everything we've done."

"I believe she will."

"Thanks for all the advice and help, Bill. It wouldn't be nearly as professional without you. It's been such fun working with you."

"You're welcome, mon très cher. I've enjoyed your company as well."

"You seem more subdued than usual. Is something wrong?" asked Marianne.

"My mind is preoccupied with something Josh said. Apparently, Lucas has decided not to pursue Ami."

"He didn't enjoy their non-date last night?"

"He told Josh that although Ami was pleasant, it was clear she was not interested in him. I'm sorry to hear that because I can't help but feel they are a good match."

"I think so, too," said Marianne.

"Well, ainsi va la vie."

CHAPTER FIFTEEN

The Investigation

"I brought the list of those Crystal possibly approached for money," said Sharon, taking a seat at the table on Ami's deck.

"Good." Ami poured Sharon a glass of lemonade. "Before we begin, I think it's important that we set ground rules."

"What do you mean?"

"Because you know these individuals, you may have a natural inclination to protect them. That won't be helpful. Honest investigation means looking the truth full in the face, even if it's ugly. Can you agree to be brutally honest about this?"

"Yes, I can," said Sharon without hesitation. "There are times in philanthropy when one must be brutal. So many causes deserve funding, but one must be discerning. I have been and can be resolute."

"Good. May I see the list?"

Sharon handed Ami a piece of fine quality stationery. The names were handwritten in legible and beautiful script.

Ami tilted her head at Sharon. "You put yourself at the top of the list?"

"I thought I should include everyone. As you are aware, Crystal did approach me."

"Let's rule you out for now and focus on the others." Ami handed Sharon back the list and flipped open her tablet. "I think the best way to approach this is for you to read a name and tell me a little something about them. I'll document your comments and ask questions as they occur to me. They may be personal, so don't be offended. Is that agreeable?"

"Yes. Next on the list is Arthur. He dated Julie, which meant a close connection to Crystal. It's possible Crystal may have uncovered some secret he is hiding."

"How long did Arthur and Julie date?"

"About four months."

"Why did they stop dating?"

Sharon paused a moment before speaking. "This is rather personal, however, not a secret. Initially, Arthur was attracted to Julie's beauty and vitality. As the relationship grew intimate, Arthur realized a challenge with the level of intimacy she preferred. Although medication is readily available, he objected to that approach. Eventually, Julie found young Jerry a more compatible partner."

"Was Arthur upset or relieved the relationship ended?"

"Very much relieved. Not only from the performance pressure, he was relieved to be free of Crystal."

"Why?"

"According to Arthur, Crystal was quite demanding. She pestered him to propose to Julie. She described plans for redecorating his house and hiring a large staff when they moved in. Her assumptions made Arthur very uncomfortable. Arthur is a man of simplicity and order. In addition, Crystal often asked him for money. He refused and reported her requests to Julie. This caused arguments between mother and daughter, further upsetting Arthur. He was not enjoying the relationship, so he orchestrated his way out."

"What do you mean?"

"Jerry is Arthur's stepson from a previous marriage. When Jerry returned from touring, Arthur invited him to accompany he and Julie to a number of events. Arthur would manage to slip away, leaving Jerry and Julie alone."

"So he was trying to set them up?"

"Yes. He was hoping Jerry and Julie would be attracted to one another. They were. When Julie told him she preferred Jerry, he happily gave them his blessing."

"And when did you and he start dating?"

Sharon smiled. "Two months later. Obviously, I had known Arthur socially for many years, but we had separate intimate circles. It was Julie's idea to set us up. I think it was her way of relieving the guilt she felt over rejecting him. She genuinely liked Arthur. They simply weren't a compatible match."

"It's obvious you and Arthur are," said Ami.

"Our first date was a dinner dance at the club. Arthur and I immediately meshed like old friends. We've been happily together ever since. Our relationship is loving and comfortable. I doubt it was Arthur who killed Crystal due to his temperament and, of course, our mutual alibi. However, if it turns out somehow he did, I would miss him terribly."

"I see you're a pragmatist."

"I've buried too many husbands not to be. Shall we move on to Jerry? He's next on the list."

"Yes. I understand his tumultuous relationship with Julie and Crystal was well observed in the community," said Ami.

"Unfortunately. I believe Jerry and Julie cared deeply for one another. The problem, of course, was Crystal. She refused to accept that Jerry was not interested in her. She was determined to marry him. I assume for his inheritance. She seemed fixated on money."

"You mentioned she asked Arthur for money when he dated Julie. Do you know if she asked Jerry?"

"I doubt it. Arthur was more approachable. He engaged Crystal in conversation in an effort to be friendly. Jerry disliked Crystal for the pain she caused Julie and for harassing him. He did his best to avoid her, especially when alone."

"Carl said Crystal called and went to Jerry's house the morning after Julie's death and that Jerry refused to answer."

"True. He was, and still is, deep in grief. I included him on my list because it's possible Crystal knew a secret about him. However, I don't believe he would have agreed to see her, no matter what her excuse for approaching him."

"Crystal's obsession with money is the theme that replays again and again. I know we're right in addressing it. It could be the key to her murder, but I don't want to get hung up on it. I believe we should look at this from several angles."

"You mean in addition to the list?"

"Yes. Matty mentioned Crystal hoarded money in various bank accounts, including a Swiss account, and investments. Do you know anything about these accounts? How much money? If she designated a beneficiary? Did she have a will?"

"Are you suggesting that someone may have killed Crystal for her assets?"

"Possibly. And it is merely a suggestion. It's one more avenue to pursue," informed Ami.

"I have no intimate knowledge of Crystal's financial arrangements. Usually one so young has not prepared a will, but if she did, I can find out for you. Her attorney, and, if I'm guessing correctly, her broker, are close acquaintance." Sharon made a note on her list. "I'll speak to them tomorrow and get back to you on that. As for the Swiss account, it is likely she would have had to designate a beneficiary upon opening it."

"Her mother?" proposed Ami.

"I doubt she would have chosen Julie. By process of elimination, I would venture to say Matty or Nancy. They were the only ones close to her."

"What about grandparents, cousins or other relatives?"

"Julie's parents died in a car accident several years ago. She has an older sister with, I believe, two children. Although Julie and her sister occasionally kept in touch through the years, they did not visit one another. I doubt Crystal ever met them. I'm sure Meg could provide you with detailed information about Julie's family. They had the sisterly bond."

"What about Jerry? He was Crystal's other obsession. Would she have left her Swiss account to him?"

"If we are following the theme of her money obsession, Jerry's wealth was his main attraction. I don't see Crystal leaving him money."

"I appreciate all the information you've provided. Marianne will be back soon and I'd prefer she not inject her opinions or overhear our conversation. She has a problem being discreet."

Sharon smiled. "Ah, possibly the reason she and Bill get along so famously."

Ami chuckled.

"I must admit I feel as if all we've done is chatter. Are we actually uncovering anything?"

"Don't underestimate chatter. It often houses important clues, and today provided us a starting point," advised Ami. "Now, our next step is to get out there and sniff around. Do you think you can arrange for lunch at the club tomorrow? Maybe I can have a tour as a prospective member. I need to observe people and, since you know everyone, you can ask the questions."

"Of course. The club is perfect for encountering many of the people on my list. Will one o'clock suit you?"

"Yes," agreed Ami.

"I'll pick you up. I must admit this is quite a gripping adventure." Sharon smiled softly.

>=<

"So, how was your investigative meeting?" asked Marianne.

"Turns out Sharon is more down to earth than we thought. She has clear insight. We discussed several of the people Crystal might have approached for money."

"Anything juicy turn up?"

"Just financial discussions at this point. We're meeting again tomorrow. How was your day with Bill?"

"Great, as always. I'm really going to miss him. I can't wait until we have everything in place. You're going to love it!"

"I'm sure I will, Dear. You and Bill have spent a lot of hours preparing. You've poured your hearts into this project and I appreciate all your hard work."

"We've been having so much fun it hasn't seemed like work. I'm hungry. What do you want for dinner?"

"Why don't we go to that seafood restaurant out by the highway? My treat! You said you read an outstanding review about it," suggested Ami.

"Ooh, I'd love it!"

>=<

"Crystal did leave a will," Sharon excitedly informed Ami once she had been escorted and enclosed in the limousine.

"Wonderful," said Ami, removing her tablet from her purse and flipping it open. "Let's record your findings. What about the will?"

"It's a very simple one. All of Crystal's assets go to Nancy."

"And the amount of those assets?"

"Close to one-half million dollars."

Ami raised her eyebrows. "She accumulated a bit for being so young. Do you know where she got her money?"

"No. However, according to her broker, she had been investing for a number of years in high risk stocks which appreciated well. Three quarters of her estate is composed of those investments."

"I would not have guessed Crystal was financially savvy."

"She wasn't. Her broker was. Apparently, she told him to invest in stocks that would provide the biggest return. He, and the rising market, performed well for her."

"Matty said Crystal used to pretend she was broke to con Julie out of money. Could Julie have given Crystal all the money for those investments and bank accounts?"

"A good bit of it, I suppose, but I doubt all of it," said Sharon.

"Do you know how she would have acquired the rest?"

"No. Crystal was not employed. I suppose one could view her a perpetual student since she registered for only a few classes each semester. I can only assume she acquired the money from an individual or several individuals."

"That brings us back to the topic of blackmail. There's a lot to uncover there. Let's put a pin in that and revisit it later. What do you know about Nancy, her beneficiary?" asked Ami.

"Little. I am more acquainted with her parents, although I do not know them well. Her father is a member of our theater guild. He's quite a good actor, given he's a Silicon Valley engineer. Somehow, one doesn't view those talents as compatible. Her mother is an orthopedic surgeon at the children's hospital. It's one of my charities. She has participated in a few of our fundraisers. She was organized, capable and pleasant. I'm afraid I have few details to contribute about Nancy. I have spoken to her briefly at events and occasionally at Julie's home."

"Tell me your impressions of Nancy from those meetings," directed Ami.

"Nancy appears a caring and reasonable young woman, quite the opposite from Crystal. She presents with far more intelligence and maturity, as well. Their friendship, which began in high school, I believe, seems anomalous. They are both only children so perhaps that forged the bond."

"I met Nancy at an art exhibit recently. I agree with your assessment of her personality. Nancy and Matty said Crystal didn't trust anyone, including them, so I doubt Nancy knew of Crystal's will. I don't believe Nancy would have killed Crystal, even if she had known. Her grief seemed genuine."

"I agree that Nancy most likely did not kill Crystal. I assume that means we are closing that avenue of exploration," said Nancy.

"Yes. We need to focus back on the blackmail angle while keeping our options open to exploring this in a whole new direction. Hopefully, a discovery at the club will provide that direction."

>=<

"You didn't mention you'd be having lunch here today," said Arthur, joining Sharon and Ami at their table.

"It was a last minute decision. Ami has been wanting to tour the club and I suggested we make it a lunch date and do it today," answered Sharon. "Was your golf game enjoyable?"

"I played well, but John still bested me, I'm afraid."

"I'm sorry," sympathized Sharon.

"It's all good fun," he dismissed. "Are you considering joining, Ami? I highly recommend the place. There's every activity you can imagine and the social

125

events are top notch," encouraged Arthur. "I suppose they filled you in on all that during your tour."

"We decided to start with lunch and tour afterward," said Sharon.

"I'm sure I'll enjoy the tour. It's a beautiful club," said Ami.

"Oh, yes," agreed Arthur. He surveyed the room. "I see John's ordered for us. See you later, my love," he said, giving Sharon's cheek a kiss. "It was lovely to see you, Ami."

"You, too," answered Ami.

>=<

"The majority of our members prefer standing appointments, but you can call the morning of, if you prefer, and we'll make every effort to accommodate you," explained Janice Sweeten, the club manager, to Ami as they completed their tour of the spa facilities.

"I recommend the standing appointment, Ami," said Sharon. "I find it so convenient. We all have them; me, Meg, Elise, Julie, Crystal. Oh, I'm so sorry," apologized Sharon.

Ami was pleased how Sharon cleverly provided the opening. "Oh, my, those were such sad tragedies," noted Ami. "It hit me hard and I only briefly knew them. I can only imagine how shocking it must have been for those of you here at the club who knew them so well." Ami looked at Janice.

"Yes. It was shocking for all of us, particularly for Lucy," said Janice.

"Did Lucy provide Julie's and Crystal's spa treatments?" asked Ami.

"No. Lucy is our dietary mixologist in our nutrition facility," explained Janice. "She creates all of the organic, nutrition drinks for our members. Crystal had a standing

126

order for our high vitamin and collagen smoothie. She had it three times a week for dinner."

"Really? I'd think one would get tired of having the same drink so often."

"The nutrition content is the same, but the ingredients are varied. Lucy is a genius when it comes to blending fruits, vegetables and supplements into delicious meals. That's why Crystal's death was so upsetting for Lucy. She had prepared Crystal a new blend the night she died."

"I hadn't heard Crystal was at the club the night she died," said Sharon.

"Oh, she wasn't. She called and asked for delivery, so Jessie dropped it off during his evening rounds."

The hair on Ami's arms bristled. So, Crystal had been delivered a new taste concoction before she died. Ami would bet that drink contained the drugs that killed her. The wine and pills on the table were a ruse.

"You have delivery? How very convenient. What else can be delivered?" asked Ami, deciding to move the conversation away from Crystal. She didn't want further inquiry to make Janice suspicious.

"We can arrange to deliver just about anything to a member, but most members enjoy coming to the club for the atmosphere and the companionship."

"Oh, I can understand that. It is beautiful here," complimented Ami. "Janice, I want to thank you so much for your time. You were very informative and I enjoyed the tour."

"It was my pleasure," responded Janice with a smile. "I look forward to welcoming you as a new member. If you have any further questions, please call."

"Thank you."

"Ami, how about a refreshing drink before we leave?" asked Sharon.

"That sounds great," said Ami.

"Thank you, Janice," said Sharon as they left.

"Great job in there. Really clever the way you brought up Julie and Crystal," complimented Ami as they exited the building.

"It popped into my mind and I said it."

"Seems you're a natural at this!"

"I have another idea."

"I'm listening," said Ami.

"There's a lovely second floor al fresco bar where Jessie often serves drinks. Would you like to have our drink there?" asked Sharon.

"I think we should, don't you?"

"Indeed," answered Sharon.

>=<

"Hi, Jessie. This is my friend, Ami Dautry, she's thinking of becoming a member."

"Nice to meet you," said Jessie. "It's a great place, even if you work here." He winked and grinned widely, but genuinely.

"It is beautiful. I had a lovely tour." Ami looked around the bar. "How come no one is here?"

"Wisely, you beat the crowd. In about an hour, this place will be hopping. Would you like the usual, Sharon?"

"No, thanks. I want something fruity and light. What do you recommend?"

"John makes a delicious peach margarita," he suggested.

"That sounds refreshing! I'd like to try that," said Sharon.

"Me, too," said Ami.

"Coming right up!" said Jessie, walking away.

"What is the plan?" asked Sharon.

"I don't have one. We'll have to wing it. We need to introduce the topic of delivery. How often do you get delivery from here?" ask Ami.

"I was aware they offered meal delivery, but have never used it," informed Sharon.

"I'm surprised they would deliver an order as small as a smoothie. Does that surprise you?" asked Ami.

"I have no knowledge of their delivery policy."

"Okay. I've got an idea. Here he comes. Just follow along."

"Ladies, I think you'll enjoy these!"

Ami took a sip as he served Sharon. "Oh, my, this is delicious. Thank you for suggesting it, Jessie."

"My pleasure. John will be pleased you like it."

"During my tour, Janice told me the club delivers. Jessie, do you know if they would deliver me peach margaritas? I'd like to relax on my deck enjoying one of these," giggled Ami.

"I doubt the club would be willing to deliver a single drink," said Sharon.

"We'll deliver anything. I often make the evening delivery run so I know firsthand."

"But not a single drink," insisted Sharon.

"Yes, I have a number of times. Mostly smoothies to Crystal. I delivered one the night…." Jessie stopped speaking and looked embarrassed. "Sorry. Shouldn't have mentioned her."

"Don't be concerned, Jessie," soothed Sharon. "I won't tell anyone."

"Thanks."

"I don't understand," said Ami.

"I suspect Jessie's been told not to mention Julie or Crystal for fear of upsetting the members. Isn't that right, Jessie?"

"Yes."

"I suppose I can understand that," said Ami. "But it seems odd to want to erase them, like they didn't exist. Doesn't it?"

"Well, we were told to be particularly careful around some members," said Jessie.

"You mean members like me and Arthur and Jerry since we were friends?"

"Yes, especially Jerry. He's normally a fun guy. We used to hang out and talk about audio equipment. We're both audiophiles. It's just now he's grieving and so we give him space. You know?"

"Yes. I know. I think that's very considerate of you," said Sharon.

"But what about you, Jessie? I'm sure hearing Crystal died on the same night you delivered to her must have upset you, too," suggested Ami. "How are you?"

"Okay now, but it freaked me out," he admitted. "Especially when the police questioned me. Chief Dawson pounded me with questions. I was scared. I mean, I was sad she died, but I was super relieved when I heard it was drugs. What if she had been shot or stabbed or something? I was there that night! Not in the house, just handed her the package when she opened the door, but, still, they could have suspected me. I'm telling you, this whole thing with Julie and Crystal has upset everybody."

"I'm sure it has. I'm sorry we upset you by talking about it," said Ami.

"It's okay, just don't tell anybody I said anything."

"Jessie, I think it would be best if we decide we never had this conversation. Agreed?" asked Sharon.

"Agreed," he answered. "Enjoy your drinks," he said, walking away.

>=<

CHAPTER SIXTEEN

The Advice

"I have some juicy gossip about you," teased Marianne over breakfast. "I've been holding off telling you because you've been preoccupied with your investigation and because it may be a touchy subject."

"I don't think I want to know," said Ami.

"I'm going to tell you anyway."

"Of course, you are. Out with it, then," said Ami.

"Lucas told Josh he's not going to pursue you anymore."

"Good," said Ami, fiddling with her grapefruit.

"Not good! You're perfect for each other!" insisted Marianne.

"You just said he's not interested in me. How is that perfect?"

"That's not what I said. I said he wasn't going to pursue you. The reason is because he thinks you're not interested in a relationship with him."

"Well, he's correct. I'm not."

"Remember when Shirley objected to your moving here and you told her Uncle George wouldn't want you to stop exploring life? Well?"

"Moving to a new place and starting a new relationship are two very different things. I have no interest in getting married again," stated Ami.

"Who said anything about marriage? It's not like in the olden days when a woman married the first man she dated." Marianne's mouth dropped open. "OMG, you've never had sex with anyone but Uncle George! Is that what this is about? Are you afraid to have sex with Lucas?"

Ami put down her grapefruit spoon and looked at Marianne. "Well, thanks a lot. That hadn't even entered my mind. Now, you've added to my reasons for not wanting a relationship."

"Oh, come on. You realize you can make whatever rules you want. Tell him sex is off the table. Stick to public places, like art shows and restaurants and the club. Bill said there are lots of dances at the club. You love dancing."

"I'm not a member."

"I thought you were going to join?"

"That was just an excuse for a tour. I have no intention of joining. The monthly membership fees are outrageous."

"Maybe Lucas is a member."

"I'm not interested. End of conversation."

>=<

"This will be quick. I just need to flick a touch of light in your left eye. That's it! It's complete," said Ami. "Would you care to see it?"

"Of course," said Sharon, getting up from her chair and walking over to the canvas. She studied it for several moments before speaking. "I wouldn't have thought a small brush stroke would have much effect, but it made it perfect." Her eyes glistened. "Thank you, Ami, you made me beautiful."

"You are beautiful! It will take about a week to dry thoroughly. I'll deliver it then."

"Just in time for Arthur's birthday. Arthur didn't want a big celebration and requested a small dinner party at the club instead. We were hoping you'd join us."

"Thank you. I'd love to."

"Wonderful. I'll have an invitation delivered to you later today. I've invited Lucas. Arthur holds him in high esteem. I understand you two are dating."

"I am not dating Lucas. Where did you hear that?"

132

“Bill told me.”

“Bill has misinformed you. Lucas and I attended an art exhibit together. It was not a date,” firmly stated Ami.

“I’m sorry I upset you,” apologized Sharon. She hesitated for a moment and then asked, “May I continue with a thought that may possibly upset you further?”

Ami sighed. “Why not?”

“I understand your husband died two years ago and you are in the process of rebuilding your life with your move here.”

“I see Bill has been very informative.”

“As one widowed woman who had to rebuild her life to another, I can attest that relationships are a natural part of that rebuild.”

“Not for me,” said Ami.

Sharon smiled. “May I ask why the idea of dating Lucas upsets you so much?”

“It has nothing to do with Lucas personally,” said Ami. “George and I shared a love that lasted over thirty years. I can’t imagine a relationship with anyone else.”

“I understand. Honestly, I do,” said Sharon. “After my first husband died, I remained alone for four years. I equated being with someone else to being unfaithful to him. Is that what you’re feeling?”

“I hadn’t thought of it that way, but I suppose so.”

“I think that is a natural phase for a lot of us widows.”

“A phase?”

“Yes. I was fortunate to have a caring mother-in-law who pushed me through it. One day, she sat me down and chided me for my solitude. Deemed it an insult to the love her son had shared with me. She challenged me to have the courage to open my heart, grab love with both hands and hold tight. Her loving gesture served me well and got me through many dark days over the years.”

"Bill told me about your husbands' deaths. I'm sorry you suffered so much grief."

"Thank you. My mother-in-law's guidance was a special gift. It taught me resilience. When each of those grievings had subsided, I understood the value of moving into love again. I'd like to pass her gift on to you, if I may?"

"I appreciate the thought, but I'm not interested in love again. My love with George was enough."

"You were fortunate to have been blessed with so many years of love. I imagine that love was essential to your happiness."

"Of course. It filled my life with joy."

"You have many years of life yet to live. Do you honestly believe George would want you to live them without the joy of love?"

Ami didn't respond for several moments, and, finally, answered softly. "No."

Sharon patted Ami's shoulder. "No need to see me out," she said. She walked to the studio door and closed it behind her.

Ami remained in her studio, alone, looking out at the ocean.

>=<

"Hello, Ami. Lovely to see you," greeted Josh.

"I'd like to take you up on your invitation. I have about an hour before I'm allowed back home. As instructed, I've left them alone and kept busy all day, and, frankly, I'm beat."

"Come into the garden and we'll have some refreshments and relax."

"Thanks. I'd love that," said Ami.

Josh led the way to the table beside a small waterfall and large patch of multi-colored flowers. "I was about to enjoy an afternoon tea tray. Or would you prefer something stronger?"

"Tea sounds wonderful," said Ami.

"Settle in. I'll be back shortly."

Ami took a deep breath and allowed her mind to float aimlessly with the trickling sound of the water.

Within short time, Josh returned with a tray filled with mini sandwiches and cakes. A waiter followed with the teapot tray.

After everything was served and the waiter had left, Ami said, "I think this is one of my favorite spots in your garden. It's peaceful. I especially love the sound of the waterfall."

"I'm so happy you're enjoying it. Do you mind if I go with you to the reveal? I'd love to see the end result."

"Oh, please do! I expect it will be lovely, judging by the photos they've shown us."

"Bill and I have a request," said Josh.

"What is it?"

"We'd like to throw you a housewarming celebration next Saturday. We'll keep it simple, just drinks and hors d'oeuvres. And we'll limit the guest list to Meg and Carl, Sharon and Arthur, Elise and Lou. I promise you won't have any disturbance to your new accessories. Our staff will cater and clean up afterward. What do you say?"

"That's lovely, but you and Bill have been more than generous already."

"We felt sad your start in your new home was marred with unpleasantness. We want to wipe that away with this celebration. Please, say yes. It would bring us such pleasure."

"I know Marianne would enjoy having guests over to see all of their designs. She's very excited about it. Thank you. Yes," agreed Ami.

"Bill will want to show it off, too. And since Marianne is leaving, we'll make it a celebration of her as well. Bill is going to miss her terribly. He's grown very fond of her."

"It's mutual. She adores him."

"I imagine you'll miss her."

"Yes, I will, but I must admit I'm looking forward to having the house all to myself."

"Understandable. And you'll be busy with your work. Elise told me she commissioned her portrait."

"Yes. I'm looking forward to working with her."

"I'm sure you'll have many requests once your beautiful portrait of Sharon is unveiled. I spoke with her today. She is passionate about it and can't wait for Arthur to see it. I understand you're attending alone. Marianne didn't want to come?"

"Mike is flying in tomorrow. They want some time alone."

"I look forward to meeting him. I assume he's staying and traveling back with Marianne?"

"Yes. They're driving to Monterey on Sunday to spend a few days with my mother before flying home," informed Ami.

"About tomorrow night," said Josh, hesitantly. "Sharon invited Lucas. Arthur admires him and they've become friends over the years. Will you be comfortable with his being there?"

"Of course. Sharon told me she invited him. Why wouldn't I be comfortable?"

"I understand things didn't go well on your outing."

"Josh, I had a lovely time with Lucas at the art exhibit. I'm sorry if he didn't."

"He did! He very much enjoyed being with you. He thought you didn't."

"I can't think of what I could have done to give him that impression, but I'm sorry he thought that."

"I'm so relieved. Is it okay if I let him know that?"

"Sure, but please stop trying to fix us up. It has nothing to do with Lucas personally. He's a fine man. I'm just not interested in a relationship with anyone."

"You're right. I have no business interfering. I'm very sorry, Ami. It's just that I love you both and got carried away. Please, forgive me?"

"Of course. You meant well. Let's forget it."

CHAPTER SEVENTEEN

The Reveal

"Ta-da!," announced Marianne, opening the door to Ami and Josh.

Josh allowed Ami to enter first and then he walked in and stood beside Bill.

Ami slowly passed through the newly created foyer designed with the beautiful screen and the healthy ficus tree. Entering the living room, she panned each section, turning as she did so. "It's more beautiful than I imagined. When you talked about adding color to neutral basics, I envisioned a bright pillow here and there. I didn't realize the accessories would have such an impact. Oh, what a beautiful orchid plant!"

"Bill remembered my telling him you liked Elise's orchids so he added it," said Marianne.

"That was very thoughtful. Thank you, Bill."

"My pleasure," he answered.

"The two of you are decorating wonders. You've made this room so…so joyful. I love every single thing in it."

"I'm so happy!" Marianne rushed to her aunt and gave her an enveloping hug.

Bill smiled broadly.

"Very nice," said Josh, patting Bill's shoulder.

"Come on, come see the guest rooms," said Marianne, leading the way.

Bill and Josh followed.

The front guest room was decorated in shades of soft green accents.

"This is a restful color combination. I love the twisted wood bedside table. It looks more tree-like than in the photo. Oh, look at the cypress bonsai on the dresser!" said Ami.

"Bill thought of it. It echoes the big cypress in the front yard you can see through this window. Don't you think?"

"Yes, it does. Thank you, Bill," said Ami.

He smiled in response.

"Wait til you see what we've done with the deck guest room!" said Marianne, running on ahead.

"The soft blues are lovely," said Ami, entering the room. "It brings the ocean in. Similar to what you did with the bonsai in the other guest room. The chaise is perfect by the window. And that chenille throw is beautiful."

"Another of Bill's ideas. He consistently one-upped my suggestions almost every time," said Marianne.

"I've been at this a lot more years, mon très cher," said Bill.

"I want you to see your bedroom, now!" said Marianne.

When they reached the bedroom, Marianne took a deep breath, flung open the door and stepped aside.

Ami's mouth fell open at the sight of a matching bed next to hers.

"Please, don't go all ballistic on me," cautioned Marianne. "It's a gift and you can't get mad at a gift." She turned to Bill and Josh for reinforcement.

"I realize Marianne overstepped, but the addition was necessary to the feng shui of the room. It's simply for furniture balance. Please don't be angry with her," implored Bill.

"Her heart was in the right place. I'm sure you realize it's a gift from love," added Josh.

Ami let out a sigh. "Of course, it was love. It's the main reason she gets away with so much."

"Do you like the color?" asked Bill, attempting to shift the focus.

"Yes. The soft yellows are sunny without being too bright. Oh, you created a cushioned reading nook near the door."

"Bill said soon it will be too cool for outside reading, and I know you've enjoyed reading on the deck before bed. So, we created this transition. You can look out at the ocean while staying warm."

"It looks very comfortable. I'm sure I'll get a lot of use out of it."

"Wait until you see what's in the closet," said Marianne, opening the door. "Party clothes!"

"You bought me clothes?"

"We made you clothes," corrected Marianne. "Remember, I took that sewing class a few years ago and Bill alters the costumes for the theater productions. The clothes are all mix and match separates so you can rewear them."

"These fabrics are lovely, but they look very expensive," said Ami. "This is too much."

"You're so tiny, it didn't take much fabric. Explain how to wear them, Bill."

Bill stepped forward. "You have a base of neutrals; black, navy, grey, ivory and white." He swung the items gently as he spoke. "There are long and short skirts, slacks, tops and jackets in a mix of fabrics. Using separates provides you with an extended wardrobe."

"And look at this flared skirt," said Marianne. "It's fitted at the waist and hips and then flares around the legs. I know you've always wanted one for dancing, but said you were too short for them because they always bunched around the middle."

"I can't believe you remembered that," said Ami. Tears filled her eyes.

"We managed to make it smooth with bias cut. Bill's idea. Tell her, Bill."

"It's a trick I learned many years ago tailoring upholstery and drapes," he said.

Marianne pulled open a drawer, "And in here are accessories in accent colors to draw attention. There are scarves and belts. Look at this gold sculpted scarf. It's like a necklace. The colorful accessories will draw attention and be remembered, so you can rewear the base outfits. It's just like what we did with your house."

"I'm overwhelmed. The clothes are beautiful. This room is beautiful. The whole house is beautiful. I don't have words enough to express my thanks to you both."

"You're very welcome," said Bill.

"So you're not mad at me?" asked Marianne coyly.

"I'm not happy about the bed, but it would be ungrateful to be mad at you after all your thoughtfulness, hard work and expense," replied Ami.

"Wonderful!" said Marianne, giving Ami a hug. "Let's go outside and celebrate with some champagne! I wasn't sure if we'd end up happy or sad once you saw the bed, so champagne seemed the perfect choice."

"I'm not sure I understand that," whispered Josh to Bill.

"Oh, champagne is what Marianne drinks when she's sad. She insists it's the perfect drink for the occasion because of the bubbles."

Josh placed his hand on Bill's arm to halt him. "Alcohol is a depressant. Not a healthy choice to mix with sadness. That's how suicides happen."

"Not to worry. The last couple weeks have convinced me she's in no danger. Her natural state is ecstatic," said Bill.

CHAPTER EIGHTEEN

The Birthday

"To Arthur! Good health and long life!" toasted John, raising his glass.

"To Arthur!" joined in the rest of the group, raising their glasses.

"Speech!" coaxed John.

"Oh, my," mumbled Arthur, standing. "I suppose I'd like to start by thanking all of you for celebrating with me. It is indeed the greatest gift in life to have good friends. One often thinks it's family, but you don't get to choose them," laughed Arthur.

Everyone chuckled along.

"An important thank you before I sit and allow you to enjoy your meal. Thank you to my darling, Sharon. At the age of seventy-five, I am fortunate to be blessed with the most loving relationship of my life. To Sharon!" said Arthur, raising his champagne glass.

"To Sharon!" echoed the group.

Sharon smiled and affectionately patted Arthur's hand when he sat back down.

Bill was seated to Ami's right. He leaned toward her and whispered, "I've known Arthur many years and this is the happiest I've ever seen him. Sharon is obviously good for him. I'm very happy for them."

"I agree," said Ami. "They have a loving connection that emanates. I feel that when I'm around you and Josh."

Bill nodded. "Yes. We've been enjoyably together for many years now. I think it's because neither of us expects the other to make him happy. I'm a great believer that happiness comes from within. We each have artistic interests that encourage our growth and bring us joy. How sad it must be to stagnate through life? I often think that unhappy people could be uplifted by artistic endeavors."

"I agree. I can't imagine my life without painting. It's my passion."

"And you excel at it. Sharon gave me a peek at the portrait. It's superb!" complimented Bill.

"Thanks. I'm really pleased with it, too."

"Getting back to couples, I assume Mike arrived safe and sound?"

"Yes. Marianne could hardly contain herself. She's acting like a recently adopted puppy."

"Haven't they been married a number of years?"

"Yes, they have. It's her mindset. You know the way she gets caught up in a current project and sort of forgets about everything else?"

"Yes. I experienced that several times during our decorating adventure," recalled Bill.

"She does it with Mike, too. Out of sight, out of mind. When he arrives, she remembers she loves him and is overjoyed. It's endearing, really."

"I'm looking forward to meeting him. He must have tremendous patience and fortitude."

>=<

"Aunt Ami certainly has found herself the perfect house and location," said Mike, walking along the rocky beach with Marianne. "I can't believe it came with a studio!"

"I know! It's like this place was made for her!"

"You and Bill should be very proud of yourselves. You did a fantastic decorating job. I don't know much about feng shui, but it feels really peaceful inside that house."

"That's the whole point!"

After the singing and candle snuffing, the waiter took Arthur's cake away to cut and plate.

Sharon stood. "I know that Arthur requested no gifts, but I have something special for him." She nodded to the maître d'.

Two waiters arrived, one with an easel the other with the covered portrait and placed them at Arthur's side.

"Arthur, would you like to do the unveiling?" Sharon asked.

Arthur stood and removed the cloth from the painting. He gasped. Recovering his voice, he announced, "It's magnificent!"

Similar comments were made by those around the table.

Sharon looked over at Ami and smiled.

"Sharon's portrait is stunning," said Jerry, he was seated to Ami's left. "I can understand now why you couldn't paint Julie from photos."

"I'm relieved to hear you say that, Jerry. I felt sad about disappointing you."

"I think I was grasping for something to help me cope with her loss."

"I know from experience that the grief process is difficult," offered Ami.

"I'm seeing a therapist to work through the guilt."

"Guilt?" asked Ami.

"I drove away that night. Maybe if I had stayed and followed Julie or if we had defied Crystal and drove home together, Julie would still be alive."

"What ifs are haunting, aren't they?"

"Yes, they are. Therapy is helping move me into a better frame of mind. The pain hasn't subsided. I think about Julie constantly. But I feel like a cloud has lifted and I'm able to see and hear more clearly."

“I understand what you mean. I’m happy you’re getting the help you need.”

“It also helps that Crystal’s dead. I don’t think I could bear her being alive after what she did to Julie.”

Ami was taken aback by his statement. “I can understand your feeling anger toward Crystal. What she did was unforgiveable. I can’t believe you’re happy she’s dead, though.”

He looked Ami squarely in the face. “Crystal was a selfish monster. She made our lives hell. She destroyed us. I’m sorry if my statement shocked you, but that’s honestly how I feel.”

>=<

“So, you found the body this close to the house?”

“I told you it was at the foot of the stairs,” reminded Marianne.

“I know you did, but I didn’t picture it being on your doorstep,” said Mike. “It must have been shocking and pretty gruesome. You sure you’re okay?”

“Of course. I’ve been so busy with redecorating the house and making Aunt Ami’s clothes, I forgot all about the murders. Aunt Ami and Sharon, that’s the rich widow I told you about, have taken on the case. So far, they’ve tied Crystal’s murder to money.”

“What do you mean they’ve taken on the case? What about the police?”

“Oh, I forgot to update you! Aunt Ami went to an art show with that hunky police chief. He still has the hots for her, but she iced him out. She said she’s not ready for a relationship, but I think she secretly likes him.”

“Is that what that bed was all about? Please, stop pushing her,” said Mike.

“I think Lucas would be a good match. Aunt Ami just needs a little nudge.”

"That sounds just like something your mother would say."

"How dare you!" gasped Marianne.

"I'm just calling it like a see it. You hate it when she butts in your life."

"Okay, you made your point. I'll leave Aunt Ami alone," conceded Marianne.

"Thank you."

"And the bed was strictly for feng shui."

"Don't even try. You should know by now you can't con me."

>=<

"I wanted to congratulate you on the portrait, Ami. It's beautiful."

"Thank you, Lucas. It helps when you have a beautiful subject."

Sharon had seated Lucas and Ami at opposite ends of the table. Ami felt it was a gesture to make them more comfortable. This was the first opportunity they'd had to speak with one another since their art outing.

Bill arose from the table. "If you'll excuse me for a moment. Please, Lucas, have a seat while I'm gone," he offered.

"Do you mind, Ami?" ask Lucas.

"Of course, not."

Once seated, Lucas leaned in and lowered his voice, "I've been wanting to speak with you about the art exhibit. I apologize if I did anything to make you uncomfortable."

"Lucas, you didn't make me uncomfortable. It seems our outing has been gossip fodder. I'd like to speak for myself. My lack of interest in a relationship has nothing to do with you. I find you an intelligent and attractive man. I enjoyed your company at the art exhibit. My decision is a personal one. I still feel an attachment to my late husband and am not ready to let that go. I hope this clears things up.”

“I appreciate your trusting me enough to share something so personal, Ami. I find it admirable that you hold such deep affection for your husband. I assure you, I’ll respect your boundaries.”

“Thank you, Lucas. I hope we can be friends.”

“Of course. Thank you for being so forthcoming,” he said, rising from the table. “Enjoy the rest of your evening.”

Bill returned almost immediately. “Are you okay?” he asked.

“Yes. Lucas and I have agreed to be friends, nothing more.”

“Thank you for telling me. I would have worked all night trying to worm it out of you.”

Ami laughed out loud.

>=<

“How was Arthur’s birthday bash?” greeted Marianne, as Ami joined them on the deck.

‘It was lovely. Arthur loved Sharon’s portrait. So did everyone else. Elizabeth Westford approached me about a couple’s portrait for her and John’s anniversary.”

“Wonderful! Was Lucas there?” asked Marianne. “Don’t answer until I run in and get a jacket. I’m cold.”

“Here,” said Ami. She slipped the satin jacket she was holding around Marianne’s shoulders.

“It won’t fit!”

“I don’t expect you to wear it,” said Ami. “Just wrap it around your shoulders?”

“Don’t you need it?”

“I’m roasting. I should have known it was too warm for satin, but it’s so beautiful I wanted to wear it.”

“And it looked beautiful on you,” said Marianne,

"Well, the chair wore it most of the evening."

Marianne pulled the sleeves up over her shoulders. "Okay, back to Lucas."

"We had a chat and cleared up all the gossip. We've agreed to be friends and nothing more."

"Did you mention you're solving his crime for him?" asked Mike.

"I see Marianne has filled you in."

"Yes, and, in my usual caring and cautious manner, I'm concerned about your safety."

"I'm perfectly safe, Mike. Sharon and I merely meet and talk about possibilities. We're in no danger."

"What's so crunchy in your jacket pocket?" asked Marianne.

"I don't know what you're talking about," answered Ami.

"Then, what is this?" asked Marianne, pulling out a folded piece of paper.

"I have no idea," said Ami.

Marianne unfolded it and read aloud, "Stay out of this or you're next."

Mike jumped up from his chair, "Stay with Aunt Ami!" he shouted, running down the stairs to the beach.

"I'll protect you," assured Marianne. "You don't need to be afraid."

"I'm not afraid, Dear," said Ami. "But I think whoever killed Crystal is."

Mike returned about ten minutes later. "No sign of anyone on the beach or out front."

"Thanks for checking, Mike," said Ami. "Let's all go in and get some sleep."

"This is a serious threat. I'm calling the police," said Mike. "Marianne, what's the number for that Lucas?"

"I'll call," said Marianne.

>=<

"Why do you think you received this threat?" asked Chief Dawson.

"I don't know," answered Ami.

"Is it possibly the result of the private investigation you and Mrs. Randall are conducting into Crystal Crestly's death?"

Marianne's eyes widened. "You know about that?"

"Yes," he answered.

"Sharon and I simply meet and talk. We haven't approached anyone we consider a suspect."

"I believe Mrs. Randall approached Crystal's lawyer and broker. I believe you questioned employees at the club."

"But they weren't suspects. We were having lunch and a tour and asked a few questions," justified Ami.

Marianne turned to Chief Dawson. "She's been holding out on me about what they've been up to and now she's holding back on you. I'll tell you what little I know. Aunt Ami and Sharon think the main suspect is someone Crystal tried to blackmail. Sharon made up a list of people she thought Crystal may have approached that had a secret to hide. They've been going through it discussing the people, but, as far as I know, they haven't settled on anyone. They discussed Nancy being the killer, since she was Crystal's beneficiary, but nixed that idea. Did you know Crystal had almost a half million in banks and investments?"

"Yes," he answered.

"Did you know about their list, too?"

"Yes."

Marianne turned to Ami. "He knows what you've been doing. Who do you think told him?"

"My first guess would be you, but since you seem surprised by it, I'll rule you out," answered Ami.

Chief Dawson turned his head away and smiled. He resumed a serious demeanor and turned back to them. "Let's discuss the party because the timing of this threat points there. Tell me who was close enough to you tonight to slip this note in your pocket?"

"Anyone could have done it. The jacket was on the back of my chair most of the evening. Just about everyone came up to me to compliment Sharon's portrait."

"Let's have summaries of those interactions, specifically comments made about Julie or Crystal."

Ami thought for a moment before speaking. "I can recall three conversations about them. The first was with Alex Sutton. He's an artist, too, so he expressed the regret and anger he felt when he'd heard of Julie's portrait being slashed. He said although he had never gotten along with Julie, he called her pushy and inconsiderate, he was sorry she died. He said Crystal had approached him for money, accusing him of killing Julie. He said he scolded her harshly before sending her away."

Chief Dawson completed his notes and asked, "And the second?"

"Jerry Robson sat next to me at dinner. He discussed processing his grief and seeing a therapist to help him through it. He made a comment about Crystal being a selfish monster and that he was relieved she was dead. When I suggested he didn't mean that, he replied he was sorry if that shocked me, but he was being honest."

"And the third?"

"That was Elizabeth Westford. She approached me about a portrait commission and mentioned how grateful she was that Marianne helped Matty get that interview. As we discussed Matty, she said she disapproved of his friendship with Crystal, noting an incident where Crystal asked Matty for fifty thousand dollars in exchange for not releasing a compromising photo of him. Apparently, when Matty told Crystal he didn't care, she threatened to get the money from his grandparents. Matty went to her and John and told them not to give Crystal money. Elizabeth said she was very angry about it and called Julie. She said although Julie was embarrassed and apologetic, she didn't seem surprised. Elizabeth got the impression this wasn't the first time Julie was told of Crystal trying to blackmail someone."

"Of the three, my bet is on Jerry," said Marianne. "He told you he was glad she was dead. And he's the one person Crystal would have invited in for a drink. It would have meant she'd won her prize. It would have been easy for him to slip drugs in her drink while she stared at him with self-satisfaction. Basic psychology."

"Whoever killed Crystal didn't need any contact with her," said Ami.

Chief Dawson stared at Ami. "Seems you and Mrs. Randall have done more than meet and talk. Would you like to explain why the killer didn't need contact with Crystal?"

Ami sighed. "The drugs were put in the smoothie Lucy prepared and Jessie delivered."

"Is that true?" Marianne asked Chief Dawson.

"I won't answer that," he said. "And everything we have discussed tonight is confidential. I don't want you relating any of this to anyone, especially Bill." He focused his gaze on Marianne.

"I promise," she said.

Chief Dawson stood up. "If you think of anything else, please call me." He turned to Ami. "I'm very relieved that you were not injured. But this isn't over. You've frightened someone. This time, they threatened you. Next time, they'll hurt you. Please, keep alert. And, above all, stop investigating."

"It was an attempt to scare me, not harm me. I feel perfectly safe."

"Someone just threatened your life," said Mike. "Maybe you don't take it seriously, but we do."

Chief Dawson turned to Mike and Marianne. "Stay close to her."

"We'll stick like glue," Marianne replied.

>=<

"Good morning. Thanks for calling us," said Bill when Marianne opened the door.

"We came to check on her. How is she taking this threat?" asked Josh.

"Not taking it seriously," Marianne answered. "Please, come in. Maybe you can talk some sense into her." She led them out to the deck where Ami and Mike were having coffee.

"Mike, this is Bill and Josh," said Marianne.

Mike stood and moved toward them.

"We've been looking forward to meeting you," said Bill, stepping forward and shaking Mike's hand.

"Yes, we have," said Josh, following suit.

"Me, too," said Mike. "Marianne's talked non-stop about you."

"We have a mutual admiration going," said Bill.

"Ami, we are relieved you're okay," said Josh.

"It was just a threat to scare me. It's nothing."

"Well, Chief Dawson doesn't think it's nothing," said Mike.

"And neither do we," said Josh. "After Mike and Marianne leave this weekend, we'd like you come and stay with us until this person is apprehended."

"That's not necessary. I'm perfectly safe."

"No sense trying to reason with her," said Marianne. "She's in her unbudgeable mood."

"Can I see the note?" asked Bill.

"Sorry, Lucas took it," said Marianne.

152

“Of course, evidence. Too bad. I was hoping I’d recognize the handwriting.”

“Printed block letters.”

“Two outs,” said Bill.

CHAPTER NINETEEN

The Clarification

"I'm leaving now to have lunch with Sharon. I'll see you later," called Ami out to the deck.

Marianne ran inside. "You can't go anywhere. We have to guard you."

"Don't be ridiculous. I'm perfectly safe at Sharon's house."

"Well, we'll walk you there."

"Most certainly not," said Ami, leaving the house.

Mike and Marianne followed her at a slight distance as she walked the five minutes to Sharon's house.

Ami turned before ringing the bell. "Okay, you've delivered me safely," she called to them. "I suggest you not stand out here for hours. Goodbye."

"Do you promise to call us when you're ready to leave?" asked Marianne.

"Sure."

"She's lying," said Marianne as she and Mike walked away. "We'll call Sharon's house and check on her after lunch."

>=<

Sharon placed her fork on her salad plate and looked over at Ami. "I owe you an apology."

"For what?" asked Ami.

"I have been briefing Arthur on our discussions. I found them exciting and wanted to share. I swore him to secrecy. This morning, Arthur confessed that, out of concern for our safety, he has been informing Lucas. After your being threatened last night, it appears he was right in doing so. However, I should not have violated our confidentiality. I'm sorry."

"Thank you for the apology. And don't worry about that threat. It says more about the killer's fear than mine."

"Ami, I think you need to take this seriously. Since we do not know the identity of the killer, you are at a disadvantage in protecting yourself."

"I think I do know his identity," said Ami.

Sharon's mouth opened, "Who?"

"Not until I'm sure. To be sure, we need to confirm he had opportunity to put the drugs in the drink," said Ami

"How do we discover that?" asked Sharon.

"We trace the drink. The drink was made by Lucy in the dietary kitchen. During my tour, we were told that area was restricted due to health regulations. Remember?"

"Yes," said Sharon. "Which means the drink had to have been tampered with after it left the dietary kitchen."

"Exactly," said Ami. "At some point, that drink was left unguarded and the killer put the drugs in it."

"So, our job is to learn the delivery protocol," said Sharon.

"Yes, specifically for that night. Did Jessie go into the kitchen for the items? Was a cart left in the hall? And what happened after he loaded it in his delivery vehicle? Did he go inside to pick up other delivery items or stop to chat with someone, leaving the food unguarded? Did he notice any members hanging around the cart or the vehicle?"

"Which means we have to talk with Jessie again," said Sharon.

"Yes, but this time in a private place. I'm guessing you're still hungry. How would you like to place a lunch order to be delivered?"

"I do enjoy their langoustine salad," said Sharon.

>=<

"Thank you, Jessie," said Sharon. "I hope you can spare a moment or do you have other deliveries?"

"You're my only delivery."

"Wonderful. Please come in and join us. We're having some lemonade in the sunroom."

"Sure," said Jessie, hesitantly. He followed Sharon.

"Hi, Jessie!" greeted Ami. She looked at his wary expression and added, "All is well, we just had an idea about the night you delivered the smoothie to Crystal and wanted to get your input."

Ami smiled at him and watched his face relax.

"Okay," he answered.

"Please, have a seat," said Sharon. She poured a glass of lemonade and handed it to him.

"You must keep confidential what we tell you. Will you agree to that?"

"Okay." His expression became cautious again.

"It's nothing illegal or dangerous. It's just confidential," said Ami.

"Okay," he said, taking a sip of lemonade.

"We think someone drugged the drink you delivered to Crystal."

His eyes grew large. "You mean I delivered the drink that killed her?"

"Yes."

"But I didn't know! I swear!"

"Jessie, relax. We know you didn't know and so do the police. You're not in any trouble. You didn't do anything wrong," assured Ami. "We just want you to help us figure out how the person got the drugs in the drink. Okay?"

"Okay. So, that was why Chief Dawson asked me all those questions?"

"Yes. He was trying to recreate the events that night. And that's what we want to do, too. All you have to do is answer a few questions. Okay?"

"Okay."

"Did you go into the dietary kitchen to get Crystal's smoothie or did you pick it up somewhere else?" asked Ami.

"There's a shelf by the door where Lucy places the pick up items. The drink was sitting there."

"Was the drink sealed or wrapped?"

"It was in a thermal bag with a tag with Crystal's name and address on it."

"Was the thermal bag sealed?"

"No, it has a pull string closure so I can take the drink out when I get to the house."

"So, the thermal bag is just to keep the drink cold during transport?"

"Yes."

"You picked up the thermal bag from the shelf by the dietary kitchen door where Lucy had placed it?"

"Yes."

"And then where did you go? Did you have other pick ups?"

"Yes. I went to the culinary kitchen and picked up a hot thermal bag for delivery."

"Did you carry the cold thermal bag with you or was it left on a cart somewhere?"

"I had it with me in the mini shopping cart I push around to pick up delivery items."

"Where was the cart when you picked up the hot thermal bag from the culinary kitchen?"

"It was with me. I wheeled it in the kitchen."

"Good. Would you say that from the time you picked up the smoothie until you left the culinary kitchen, anyone trying to tamper with the drink easily could have been seen by you?"

"Yes. No one touched the drink during that time."

"That's helpful to know. Where did you go after you left the culinary kitchen?"

"I went to my jeep and put the thermal bags in the thermal boxes."

"Tell me about the boxes."

"They are mounted to the back of the jeep. There's a hot box and a cold box."

"Do they have a latch of some kind?"

"No latch. Tops open like a cooler. They're deep so nothing can fall out."

"What did you do after you put the deliveries in the thermal boxes?"

"I delivered them."

"Did anyone talk with you before you drove off or stop you while you were driving out of the club?"

"Oh, I see what you mean. Chief Dawson asked me about that, too."

"What did you tell him?"

"I told him about Alex Sutton stopping by the jeep before I left. We chatted for a few minutes. I used to help him paint scenery. We hadn't seen each other in awhile so we were catching up."

"Who else stopped by?" asked Ami.

"Nancy and Paul chatted with me for a few minutes. They were going to the bar for a drink. And Keith and Jerry gave me a shout out as they walked by on their way to the tennis courts."

"Did you leave the jeep at any time before you drove off?"

"Well, I ran over real quick to tell Kelly our date was being pushed back because of the deliveries."

"Could you see the jeep from where you and Kelly were talking?"

"No. She was inside, but I was only gone a couple of minutes." His face went grim. "That must have been when someone tampered with the drink."

"It's okay, Jessie. You would have had no way of knowing. It's not your fault," reassured Ami. "Now, this is an important point. Do you remember mentioning to anyone that you were delivering a drink to Crystal?”

“Well, yes. I told Kelly and I told Nancy and Paul.”

“Do you remember anyone being around that might have overheard you when you were speaking?”

“I guess someone could have overheard. People are always standing around or walking by. I’m really sorry.”

“Jessie, none of this is your fault. You’ve been a great help. I want you to help further by going to Chief Dawson as soon as you leave here and telling him everything you told us. Will you do that?”

“Sure. But I’ve already told him all of this when he questioned me. Do you want me to tell him again?”

“Did you tell him about mentioning the delivery for Crystal and leaving the jeep to talk with Kelly?”

“Yes.”

“Good. Then he probably knows who did it, too,” said Ami.

“Who?”

“I’m sorry, but I can’t tell you right now. You must promise that you will not tell anyone you spoke with us, not even Kelly. This is very confidential. After the person is arrested, you will be able to tell people that the information you provided helped Chief Dawson solve this crime.”

“It did?”

“You did. Do you promise confidentiality?”

“I promise.”

Sharon walked him to the door.

>=<

“I see you two are deep in conversation,” said Arthur entering the sunroom. Jerry Robson was with him. “Ami, how lovely to see you.”

"Hello, Arthur, Jerry," said Ami, rising to leave.

"Jerry and I are off to the club for a drink. We stopped by to see if you'd like to join us. Please don't leave, Ami. You're invited as well."

"Thanks, but I'm expected home. Mike and Marianne are waiting for me. Oh, Jerry, I put those photos of Julie on a flashdrive for you. Feel free to stop by on your way to the club, if you want."

"Thank you for doing that. Yes, I will stop by for it," he replied.

"See you later, then," said Ami.

>=<

"Aunt Ami, you've been gone all afternoon. I'm so relieved you're home," said Marianne, running to the door to meet her. "I knew you were lying when you agreed to call us."

"As you can see, I'm safe and sound. Hi, Mike!"

"Hi, Aunt Ami."

"What would you and Mike like to do about dinner tonight? I can take you to that seafood restaurant you like?"

"We decided we wanted to stay in tonight. We picked up some steaks to grill. And we stopped by the bakery and got a dozen of those mini chocolate éclairs you like. I made a big salad. Everything's in the fridge for later."

"That all sounds wonderful. Why don't we have a drink out on the deck. I have some information I'd like to share with you."

>=<

"Oh, Marianne, will you get that?" asked Ami at the sound of the doorbell. "It's probably Jerry Robson

160

coming to pick up the flashdrive. It's in my studio. Will you please send him there?"

Marianne escorted Jerry to Ami's studio and remained standing at the doorway.

"Hi Jerry!   Here's the flashdrive," said Ami, handing it to him. "Do a have a minute to talk?"

"Just a minute. Arthur and Sharon are waiting for me."

"Marianne, you can leave now," instructed Ami.

Reluctantly, Marianne walked away.

"I'll get right to the point. I know it was you who put the drugs in Crystal's smoothie," said Ami. "And I know it was you who left that note in my jacket."

"I don't know what you're talking about."

"When you and Keith walked by Jessie on your way to the tennis courts, you overheard him tell Nancy and Paul that he was delivering a smoothie to Crystal. I think that's when the idea popped in your head to put the drugs in the drink. I think you made some excuse to Keith to leave the court and when Jessie left the jeep to go speak with Kelly, you crushed up several of your Percocet and shook them into the drink. You carry them around with you due to your shoulder injury."

"That story is absurd. Everyone knows Crystal died from mixing wine and drugs."

"Yes, about the wine and drugs. My guess is you thought it fortuitous when Crystal called just as you were returning to the court. Instead of letting it go to voice mail like you did her many other calls, this time, you answered. You agreed to see her. You told her to prepare for your visit by pouring the wine and putting one of Julie's Vicodin into your glass. I'm guessing you used your shoulder pain as the excuse for the drug cocktail. Of course, you had no intention of joining her. You had already poisoned her smoothie. You were having her set the stage for her cause of death."

"Is that what you and Sharon were doing today? Making up crazy scenarios about Crystal's death? I think you both need to find healthier hobbies."

"You can deny to me, Jerry, but your denial won't work with Julie. Julie may be dead, but she knows what you did. It must hurt her deeply that you killed her daughter. You've both suffered so much, and you're both still suffering."

Jerry lowered his head and exhaled deeply. "I can't bear anymore." After a few moments, he looked up at Ami. "I never planned to drug her. It sort of happened on its own. When I heard Jessie say her name, the anger and hate I felt for her exploded inside me. All I could think about was how she killed my darling Julie. And, then, I thought how easy it would be to put the Percocet in her drink. I suppose the rest follows much the way you said. All of it has become a blur to me." He exhaled deeply. "So, what now? Are you going to go to the police?"

"She doesn't need to. I'm right here," said Chief Dawson, coming up behind Jerry and clipping on the cuffs.

>=<

The table was filled with desserts. Josh had helped Marianne plate the éclairs and the miniature pies he and Bill had brought over.

Lucas poured each of them a glass of an exceptional port. His contribution to the gathering.

Marianne lifted her glass. "I want to thank Lucas for arriving in time this afternoon to save Aunt Ami."

"Thank you, but it wasn't like that at all," informed Lucas. "Ami called, told me about the conversation with Jessie and that she planned to confront Jerry when he stopped by for the flashdrive. We agreed I would stand by and witness their discussion."

"Lucas already had him under surveillance," said Ami. "And saving was never an issue. I felt certain Jerry was not going to hurt me."

"So you already suspected him?" Marianne asked Lucas.

"The smoothie container we found in Crystal's trash had tested positive for the drugs in her system so we knew immediately the wine was a set up. That allowed us to focus on opportunity for putting the drugs in the drink. As for motive, after we ruled out all of the people Crystal had approached for money, the logical conclusion was the one who would benefit some other way from Crystal's death."

"And the benefit from Crystal's death for Jerry was punishing her for killing Julie?" asked Marianne.

"Yes."

"I'm shocked at Jerry doing something like that," said Josh. "Is he still in jail?"

"He's been released on bond," said Lucas.

"Aunt Ami, what made you suspect him?" asked Mike.

"It was seeing the hatred in his face when he spoke of Crystal at Arthur's birthday," explained Ami. "That's when I knew, and, inadvertently, showed my suspicions."

"So that's why he slipped that note into your jacket," said Mike.

"I don't condone what he did, but I do feel sympathy for him," said Josh. "It must have been too painful for him that his loving Julie was dead and that wretched Crystal was still alive."

"He can afford the best lawyers, so they'll probably get him off on temporary insanity. After all, he hadn't planned it ahead of time and he was seeing a therapist for his grief," said Marianne.

"He was sane enough to try to cover it up with the wine and drugs. No matter how wretched she was, he did not have the right to take Crystal's life," said Ami.

"You realize the trial will be a circus," noted Bill. "He's somewhat of a tennis celebrity so public interest will be high. We'll be overrun with gawkers and press. They'll be swarming all over us, asking questions."

"All of which you'll relish," said Marianne.

"Ah, I shall miss you, mon très cher."

CHAPTER TWENTY

The Housewarming

Marianne thoroughly enjoyed giving the guests a full tour, and filling them in on how special pieces had been creatively selected.

Josh had instructed his staff that serving of food was limited to the deck, to eliminate spills or debris marring Ami's pristine home.

"All of the accessories and fabrics are lovely," said Elise walking back to the living room with Ami and Lou. "And the feel in each of the rooms is peaceful and uplifting. Bill and Marianne did a fantastic job."

"Did you notice that Bill added an orchid plant because I mentioned I liked yours?"

"Yes, I noticed that. I'm thankful Bill and Josh arranged this party for you. It erases all the bad energy from before."

"It's important to Elise that this is a happy home for you," said Lou.

"I'm very happy here, Elise," assured Ami.

"Aunt Ami, come see the surprise Bill has created for your deck," called Marianne.

Ami, Elise and Lou walked out to the deck where Bill, Marianne and some of the other guests were looking at the plans he had laid out on the table.

The remainder of the guests joined them and gathered around the table.

"It's a garden!" said Marianne.

"You mentioned the pleasure you get from my garden, so I wanted to gift you with a garden space to enjoy here on your deck."

"Bill, really, you and Josh are far too generous."

"Think of this as another excuse to get my hands in soil."

"Then, I feel I should warn you, I'm not a very attentive gardener. I often forget to water."

"Not to worry. The automatic drip system takes care of that."

"Look, here," said Marianne, pointing to the plan. "The garden grows in the rock bed already surrounding your deck. Bill is going to make it look like the plants are growing there naturally."

"All of the plants are perennial and contained," said Bill. "You won't need to do anything, but enjoy."

"I couldn't ask for a more exceptional garden! I'm sure it will bring me much enjoyment," said Ami. "Thank you so very much."

"It's my pleasure."

Josh raised his glass in toast. "To Ami and this beautiful home that Marianne and Bill have lovingly decorated. We warmly welcome you to our community, Ami. May you be blessed with many happy years here!"

"Amen!" said Meg. "I knew this was Ami's house the minute I met her."

"I remember you saying those exact words," said Ami.

"Honey, I always know."

>=<

Ami hugged Mike and Marianne goodbye. "Safe trip back," she said.

"I'm really going to miss you," said Marianne, giving her aunt one last hug.

"I'll miss you, too, Dear," said Ami.

"Try to stay out of trouble," called Mike as he got into their rental car.

Ami stood on the sidewalk, watching them drive off. She felt a tinge of sadness. Then, she turned and began walking up the path to her front door. Her house seemed to smile a warm greeting. She went inside and stood in the foyer, gazing around the room and appreciating all she saw. "Alone at last, lovely home," she said aloud. "Let's begin our peaceful life together."